Also available in the Rediscovered Classics series

Lodore, by Mary Shelley

The World's Desire, by H. Rider Haggard and Andrew Lang

REDISCOVERED CLASSICS

The WOMAN *in* BLACK

M. Y. HALIDOM

UNION
SQUARE
& CO.

NEW YORK

UNION SQUARE & CO.

NEW YORK

UNION SQUARE & CO. and the distinctive Union Square & Co. logo are trademarks of Sterling Publishing Co., Inc.

Union Square & Co., LLC, is a subsidiary of Sterling Publishing Co., Inc.

This 2022 edition published by Union Square & Co., LLC

A Note on the Text: This book was first published in 1913 and reflects the attitudes of its time. Accordingly, editorial changes have been made to remove certain instances of prejudicial language, but for the most part this classic work is reproduced as originally published.

ISBN 978-1-4549-4718-9
ISBN 978-1-4549-4719-6 (e-book)

Library of Congress Control Number: 2022940613

For information about custom editions, special sales, and premium purchases, please contact specialsales@unionsquareandco.com.

Printed in Canada

2 4 6 8 10 9 7 5 3 1

unionsquareandco.com

Interior design by Gavin Motnyk
Image credit: ZABIIAKA Oleksandr/Shutterstock.com (interior icons)

CONTENTS

CONTENTS

The
WOMAN
in
BLACK

INTRODUCTION

Sir Ashleigh Carruthers was the son of a country squire who lived in Midlandshire, where his family had resided for generations in a venerable pile that appeared to defy the ravages of time, and was called Tudor House. The death of his father had occurred some months after the son had reached his majority. He was a young man of active mind and restless body, and the prospect of the humdrum existence of a country gentleman, with its daily monotonous round of commonplace duties and the society of his bucolic neighbours, offered little attraction to him. His mother, who had died some years before her husband, had often expressed a wish that Ashleigh should marry early in life some lady of suitable age and position, and settle down. His father had expressed the same desire, and had gone so far as to call his son's attention to certain families with daughters, with one of whom he might form an alliance in every way desirable; in fact, he was never tired of pointing out to his son the advantages and desirability of keeping up the family name.

Ashleigh Carruthers was of a romantic and sanguine temperament, and felt a passionate desire to live a little for himself as well as for the family name; in short, he wanted to see and know something of the world and humanity, and to live a life outside the narrow surroundings which had cramped his existence for so many years. Nothing could be more repugnant to him than the idea of settling down before he had felt and known the bitter and sweet of life, like the ordinary cut-and-dried Philistine. Such a life might suit a mild young curate, brought up by a maiden aunt, who would be content to bury himself in the country and vegetate from youth to age, immersed in his parochial duties; but it would not do for a man of active mind and ardent aspirations like Carruthers.

He chafed at the social restraints that were part and parcel of his position, and sighed for a life of travel and adventure, with its accompanying light and shadow of pleasure and pain; in fact, he considered anything would be better than the wearisome, deadly routine of his present existence, which seemed to him like that of a purring cat, on a thick hearth-rug, before a clear fire.

He had not tasted the wonderful draught of life for which his soul thirsted, and yet his friends wanted him to commit the suicidal act of early marriage.

But the reader, whom we want to take an interest in the character and career of our hero, has a right to be able to picture the man physically as well as mentally. Ashleigh Carruthers was six feet high, square and broad-shouldered, his nose was long and broad at the base, with large sensitive nostrils; his mouth was quite big enough, his lips straight, but full and rather prominent, his chin was square and pronounced, the jaw indicated determination and ready energy. His eyes were blue-grey, well set under straight, thick eyebrows; the complexion was sanguine; and the well-formed, compact head was covered by closely curling fair hair; the lower part of his face was finished off by a closely cut beard and full moustache. Ashleigh Carruthers was not a sentimental, poetical-looking man; but his appearance was full of virility, and, if we may use the term, masculinity; and underneath the fierceness and strength there were, to the keen observer, clear indications of tenderness and enthusiasm. He would be difficult to excite and subdue; but when warmed to real affection he would never change or cool. We must mention his voice: it was a fine baritone, full of manly vibrations, and admirably modulated; but, perhaps, the greatest charm of the man was his unconsciousness, and the entire absence of personal vanity.

When the days of mourning for his father's death were over and Ashleigh had entered into possession, there were great speculations and greater expectations throughout the county as to which lady would fall the happy lot of ultimately becoming the mistress of Tudor Manor and the wife of the good-looking owner. Taking into consideration his family, his property, and his personal qualities, there was not in the county a better match than he.

As a matter of course, invitations poured in from all sides, and many a matchmaking mamma had already, in imagination, secured him for her eldest unmarried darling. The young squire was, however, of a rather reserved nature, and preferred hunting to being hunted, and was soon set down as proud and unsociable because he did not care to be hail-fellow-well-met with every featureless nonentity to whom he had the bad luck to be neighbour. Ashleigh Carruthers had a heart, but he did not wear it on his sleeve. He held aloof from as many parties and public meetings as he decently could. This conduct did not and could not add to his popularity.

At last, however, he got tired of his own company; and, then, to the delight and astonishment of all, accepted the invitations of his neighbours, and, as a change from solitude, enjoyed their society. He was always eagerly welcomed, and not being by temperament cold to the attractions of the opposite sex, he made himself a favourite without difficulty, and was soon described by those to whom he paid attention as the most charming of men, possessed of perfect manners, an easy flow of amusing conversation, and an appearance so attractive as to be almost irresistible.

So far all seemed to be progressing satisfactorily, and the hopes of many an anxious mother, with daughters to marry, appeared to have a good chance of realization; but as week followed week and month followed month and no proposal followed, a marked change was discernible in the attentions paid by the squire to the young ladies with whom he had flirted so easily and naturally, for Ashleigh, although young and inexperienced, had an instinctive knowledge of the world which made him perfectly aware of the witching wiles of astute mothers and the hardly less clever daughters, and drew back just at the critical moment when it was expected that the momentous question was ripe for utterance.

The interested mothers had an informal meeting, at which was discussed the question of how this young squire, who so easily eluded all their most carefully elaborated plans, could be brought to the point.

Ashleigh was master of that invaluable gift, a sense of humour; and saw through the subtle devices that were used for his capture, and was much amused by them. We are sorry to confess that he was hard enough even to take a malicious pleasure in paying extra attention to some girl he cared nothing for, in the presence of her mother and, very soon after, doing the same to another; but not one word of love and still less of marriage passed his lips.

"This has gone too far," said one elderly lady to another. "It is quite time he declared himself to someone."

"And he will have to do so, or I'll know the reason why," broke in a plethoric middle-aged man, the son of a prosperous butcher, who had overheard the remark and had himself a large family of daughters.

"I call the squire's conduct perfectly outrageous—yes, outrageous and dishonourable," he added with emphasis, as he excitedly mopped his red face with a bandana handkerchief. These remarks were made at a county ball, and this worthy gentleman, a member of the borough council and an aspiring local magnate, had just emerged from the refreshment room.

"Hush, my dear, not so loud!" whispered his equally plethoric and gaudily dressed wife, who sat fanning her red face next him. "He will hear you!"

"So much the better," blurted out her irresponsible husband. "I wish—" Then, however, the band striking up *forte,* drowned the rest of Mr. Blogg's sentence, while Sir Ashleigh coolly advanced and claimed the hand of the prettiest of the ex-butcher's daughters for the commencing waltz, carrying her off on his arm under the short but admirably coloured nose of her astonished and indignant father.

"Consummate puppy!" muttered an invidious aspirant to the hand of pretty Miss Blogg, as he gazed ruefully at the pair. The ball was kept going with vigour till the small hours of the morning, and wound up with Sir Roger de Coverley.

It is needless to descant on the sensation that the County Ball made in the dead-and-alive town of Little Fuddleton, or how for the next six months nothing was discussed but as to how Miss-so-and-so, the belle of the season, looked in her ball dress of white satin, trimmed with lace; or, old Mrs. Somebody-else in her quaint, old-fashioned gown.

"Such a caution, my dear! and, then, that odious, always flirting and never proposing squire; but there, my dear, let us leave him to his own devices, for he evidently means nothing honourable."

"He doesn't seem to be a marrying man," meekly suggested the plain Miss Stubbs, who, poor girl, knew she had no chance of winning such a matrimonial prize as Sir Ashleigh, and could, therefore, afford to be charitable.

"Nonsense about his not being a marrying man!" retorted her plainer mother. "All men who are worth anything are marrying men. He ought to be pre-eminently so in his position. More shame for him, then, if he isn't a marrying man, that's all I can say!"

"But surely, mother, he is at liberty to remain unmarried, if he likes," remarked her daughter, disinterestedly.

"At liberty, do you say!" exclaimed Mrs. Stubbs. "Ah! that's where it is. These men with their notions of liberty! Bah! a set of libertines, all of them!"

With this summary judgment, which we respectfully offer for the consideration of all hard-hearted and obdurate bachelors, we take respectful leave of Mrs. Stubbs.

• • •

CHAPTER I

THE SQUIRE AT THE FRONT

It was in the year 1900, towards the close of the Boer War in South Africa, when our troops had pitched their laager before ——— during one of the periods of wearisome inaction which were so trying to our men, that an officer in khaki sat at the opening of his tent, in the early morning, upon an empty biscuit box, his revolver by his side, and rifle and bandolier, containing cartridges, slung up inside.

Before him stretched a panorama of wild, hilly country, stony and treeless. He had just finished his breakfast of tinned meat and biscuit, washed down by a pannikin of coffee, while a servant, near at hand, tended the camp kettle. At some distance off, his horse was being groomed by his servant. Three other officers shared the tent with him, but at that moment they were on duty and he was alone. Sir Ashleigh Carruthers had been through some hard work, and the marks of anxiety and privation were visible on his countenance. The crows' feet had begun to show in the corners of his eyes, and he was considerably thinner than when we first made his acquaintance as a young man who flirted, not wisely, but too well. But although the cheekbones stood out and the face was hollow and the bony structure of his frame more apparent, added dignity and energy were displayed in his countenance, which, to many observers, would increase the attraction of his appearance. All the latent resources of his nature had been developed; and there was a keenness of expression in his eyes, due to his position of danger from an apparently never sleeping enemy, which had brought to perfect ripeness all the natural vigour and determination of his name. He was now Captain Carruthers, VC, and had served his country from the opening of the war, had been engaged in many a tough encounter with the enemy, and bore the marks of his foes in severe wounds in the knee and shoulder, and lighter ones on various parts of his body. This life suited the active and daring spirit of Ashleigh Carruthers, and when this chapter opens, he was thoroughly bored at the long period of enforced inaction, and having nothing to do, his thoughts wandered to home. His home? Well, in name and long association it was so; but what had ever made it so in reality? He had no relations living except two married sisters, and a few distant members of his family who were all now dispersed. In fact, Carruthers was quite alone in the world. To make a real home there must, first of all, be love, friendship, family ties, and agreeable associations. He was only the temporary owner of an ancestral hall, a master of many acres, the possessor of a considerable fortune; but there was no one to share it with him and thus double its value.

The one thing needful to all real happiness was wanting—true and devoted love. He felt himself far more at home on the wild, open veldt, with the stimulating dangers and privations of a soldier's life, than in the drawing-rooms of his neighbours in the vicinity of Little Fuddleton, listening to their inane gossip and petty scandal. What would the fair girls he had flirted with say to him now? Would they recognise his bronzed and worn face and bony form?

Whilst thus idly musing on the past, he absently took up a newspaper and carelessly scanned its columns, when an announcement met his eye that caused him to start with astonishment.

"What is this?" he muttered, and then proceeded to read in a low tone:

"May, the tenth, at the church of Holy Trinity, by the Rev. Samuel Tithnot, the Hon. Vincent Cholmondeley to Alice Sybil Marjoribanks, daughter of Sir William Marjoribanks, Bart., of Steepleton Hall, Midlandshire."

"Well, well," he murmured. "There's another good fellow taken in and done for. A better friend never lived. In fact, he is the only friend I ever had—and now he's lost to me!"

At that moment a letter was brought to Ashleigh by his servant. He took it, and, when the man had gone, exclaimed, "As I live, here is a letter from the poor fellow! Let me see what he says." He tore open the letter, and read as follows:

Dear old friend Ashleigh—

After so long and culpable silence on my part, I am really at a loss to begin, or know how to break to you the astounding news I have to impart.

I usually like to plunge *in medias res* without any beating about the bush; but I fear, in the present case, that should this letter reach you when you are mounted, the shock might knock you off your horse. Therefore, prepare for a blow. Do you remember, my friend, in the good old days (or the bad old days) when we were two cynical bachelors, disgusted with life before either of us knew what it was, how we used to abuse the fair sex in good round terms as an altogether inferior set of beings, fit only to be locked in a harem, to loll on ottomans and feed on peaches all day? How we used to censure their frivolity, their feebleness, their fickleness, their inanity, their extravagance, their heartlessness and want of principle, until we left them without a single virtue while we vaunted ourselves lords of the creation, possessed of all the qualities which they so manifestly lacked?

I repeat, do you remember all this conceited and arrogant nonsense, and also how we mutually resolved never to marry, deeming ourselves too precious to be thrown away on any woman? And yet— will you believe it—I, even I, your old college chum, the quondam railer and reviler of the sex in general, have at last, in my turn, but not without many a struggle—must I admit it?—succumbed to the seductive influence of one of the opposite sex, the fairest, the daintiest, the purest, the most lovable on the whole earth. Her voice is the softest music to my ears, her movements the most graceful and dignified. There is poetry in the very folds of her dress, as she sweeps across the room with that indescribably beautiful and undulating motion of hers, like some ethereal being who has descended from a higher sphere. Her eyes are deep as the blue of the ocean, her teeth like pearls gathered by the hands of mermaidens from its bottomless depths, her lips of pure coral, and her breath like the perfume of a garden of roses. Her feet—

here Captain Carruthers paused to ejaculate: "Is the fellow quite off his head? Has he gone clean daft? Oh, my poor friend, you must be far gone, indeed! A man like you, too! Who could even have dreamed it? To think what the best of us may come to?"

Then he perused the letter for a long time in silence; but soon resumed reading it aloud.

In short, there is only one thing wanting to enhance the happiness I enjoy, and that is the presence of my old friend Ashleigh to shed the light of his countenance over our happy home to the end that he may behold a true picture of matrimonial felicity as manifested in the life of his college chum, with the hope that he may renounce his former prejudices against marriage, and finally settle down with—

"Damn settling down!" exclaimed the indignant captain. "That idea is repugnant to me, and always will be. It suggests the prosiest, dreariest, most abject moral and intellectual suicide."

Then, thrusting the letter into one of his pockets, he proceeded to cut up some tobacco with his penknife, rolled it in the palms of his hands, and having thus prepared it to his satisfaction, he filled a short briar-root pipe with the pungent herb and struck a light. "Ah, that's a little better!" he muttered after the first puff or two.

"Nothing but this could have steadied my nerves after that idiotic letter. Happy, is he? but it's early yet. Only a few days after the wedding. Let him wait a bit. He'll soon be telling a different tale, I warrant. "Well, poor fellow, I'm sure I hope he will be happy with all my heart, for if ever a man deserved to be, he does. I'll go and see him, hanged if I don't, and be introduced to this paragon of a wife, when the war is over! God grant I may not prove a hostile element to their happiness, a drop of poison in their cup!"

Here he relapsed into silence, and was soon lost in thought. At length, as he was knocking the ashes out of his pipe, he saw his three brother officers, who shared his tent, returning. He rose to meet them, and some desultory conversation ensued.

It seemed to be their opinion that the war was very near its end; and it was not many weeks after this talk that Captain Carruthers and his three companions found themselves among the passengers on board the S.S. —— on their way home.

• • •

CHAPTER II
AT HOME AGAIN

N othing had ever so much surprised the inhabitants of Little Fuddleton and its neighbourhood as the sudden determination of Sir Ashleigh Carruthers to abandon the comfortable home and position that he had lately inherited, with its accompanying ease and comfort, for a life of danger and privation. "It is inconceivable, my love," said a portly matron to her marriageable daughter, "that a man in his position, with everything around him to make life worth living and after all we have been doing to keep him at home, and I am sure we did our best, should fly in the face of Providence, throw up all his friends and against their joint advice persist in his own course. He is, to say the least, a very perverse man—very."

"Still, if he obeyed the call of duty, mother," pleaded the daughter.

"Rubbish! Don't talk to me about the call of duty!" interrupted her mother. "I have a notion that duty begins at home. There are other duties for a man in his position in the country besides risking his life on the battlefield. There are plenty of others ready to do that; impecunious men, soldiers of fortune, and the like, but why a man of his stamp should want to meddle in military matters is a puzzle to me."

"Why, mother, even princes go to battle," rejoined the daughter.

An inarticulate sound of contempt by the mother terminated the conversation.

Sir Ashleigh had been away three years and was almost forgotten; but when a newspaper one day informed the countryside that the war was at an end and peace had been declared, it was natural people who had known and heard of Sir Ashleigh should recall him to their minds, and, in addition, that many mothers and daughters should feel a more or less tender interest in his return, safe and sound.

Would it be worth while in that case to re-weave meshes in which they had already tried to enclose him? Most likely he would now be more inclined to settle down; he had had his experience of danger and privation; and, perhaps, the prospect of settling and submitting to the tender ministrations of a charming and affectionate wife would prove more attractive.

At length the day dawned for the arrival of the local hero.

Several of the neighbouring magnates, amongst whom were the vicar and his wife, assembled on the platform to meet and welcome him home. As the train steamed in, slowed and stopped, the door of a carriage opened, and a tall, thin man, bearded and bronzed, dressed in khaki, stepped out, and was effusively welcomed by a score of his former acquaintances. He had neither expected nor desired such an ovation, for, being a retiring and reserved man, he had given no notice of his coming, and hoped to steal upon them all unawares. But Dame Rumour, whose tongue will clack, had been too much for him, and his desire was defeated. The vicar proceeded to monopolise our hero and insisted on driving him home in his carriage.

"You see, Sir Ashleigh," he observed, "that it was impossible you should be permitted to steal a march upon us as you evidently wished. You are too important a personage to be allowed to return like an ordinary man."

"Yes, indeed," broke in the vicar's wife, "the interest which we all take in Sir Ashleigh and his movements renders that quite impossible."

"Well, I'm sure I ought to feel very pleased and proud to find myself the centre of so much unlooked-for attention," said the captain, trying to acknowledge his thanks for what he least of all desired. "Ah, here we are!" he exclaimed, as the gates of Tudor Hall stood before him, "pray, step in and have a look at the old place; I am anxious to see how things have been going on during my absence."

"Oh, I should like it beyond all things!" said the vicar's wife.

The three left the carriage and were soon inside Tudor Hall. Two old servants, a man and his wife, who had been left in charge during the Squire's absence, having heard nothing of the reports afloat in the village about their master's return, opened their eyes with astonishment as they saw the arrival of the vicar's carriage and Sir Ashleigh alight.

"Well, Somers," said Sir Ashleigh, "you are surprised to see me again, eh?"

"Ay, Sir Ashleigh, I be surely!" said the man.

"And you, too, Mrs. Somers?" said the captain to the old woman. "Lord, love you, Sir Ashleigh—yes; it's taken all the breath out of me a'most, and kind of a knocked me all of a 'eap like," she returned.

"Well, neither of you evidently ever expected to see me again; but now that I am back safe and sound, do you think you could manage to give us all a cup of tea?" inquired Sir Ashleigh.

"Well, Sir Ashleigh, we'll do our best." And the old couple, after showing them into a room which commanded a view of the garden and park, retired.

The vicar and his wife, after glancing at the old family portraits on the wall, were soon seated, and the lady's tongue began to demonstrate its wonderful activity and staying power.

"What adventures you must have had during the long time you have been away, Sir Ashleigh! What delightfully thrilling things you will have to tell us! Well, I suppose you must long for a little rest now, and will be more ready to settle down steadily to the useful and pleasant life of a country gentleman like your dear good father before you. Now, do you know what I should do if I were in your position?"

"Well, what would you do?" enquired the captain carelessly.

"Why, first of all," proceeded Mrs. Graves, "I should look very closely and carefully around me for some really nice girl; don't be too particular about money, if she is the right sort, clever, pretty, and amiable, and marry her. You must make up your mind to marry some day—you really must, you know—all men in your responsible position do. It's only right; the county expects it of you."

At this moment, old Mrs. Somers entered, placed the tea things, and retired.

"And so, I am to marry to please the county, eh? Good, very good! Ha! ha! ha!" and Ashleigh roared with laughter. When he had sufficiently recovered himself to be able to articulate, he continued:

"I've been hitherto sufficiently simple to think that men married to please themselves."

"Well, Sir Ashleigh," said the lady, rather put out of countenance by the boisterous laughter of the squire, "I don't, of course, mean to exactly say—"

"My dear," interrupted the vicar, who, like many others in his position, had a very shrewd knowledge of how to make the best of both worlds, and especially of the one in which he occupied a very pleasant position, "don't you think you had better leave Sir Ashleigh to manage this matter for himself? He will doubtless go the way of the majority in due course. All I can say at present is that, when he has chosen his future partner for life, I shall be very happy to officiate."

"Now, I'll be bound that Mrs. Graves has someone in her mind's eye already," said Ashleigh, with twinkling eyes.

"Well, Sir Ashleigh," she said, with that half shy and half mysterious smile so common to ladies affected with the terrible disease of match-making, "I may know several very nice and very superior girls in our parish who would make unexceptionable wives. There is one in particular, an exceedingly charming girl whom I happen to know"—here she leaned towards the squire, and whispered in his ear—"is dying of love for you."

"Dying to be mistress of Tudor Hall, rather. Ha! ha! ha! Poor girl, I pity her!" laughed the squire.

"Not any more tea, thank you!" Then, turning to her husband, who had sense of humour enough to enjoy the scene between his

put-everyone-right-wife and his strong-willed host, she said rather
icily, "I think, my dear, we had better think of returning home. Goodbye, Sir Ashleigh! So glad to see you home again safe and sound. I hope
we shall see a good deal of each other in the future."

Sir Ashleigh accompanied his visitors to their carriage, and after
he had closed the door upon them, said to himself: "The same old
game! Why can't such women leave a man alone? When I do want to
marry, I will let the woman I care for know it.

•••

CHAPTER III
THE SQUIRE BORED

◇

The next morning, after bath and breakfast, both of which the captain enjoyed thoroughly, he lit his briar-wood pipe, which had been his constant friend and companion through many a bivouac on the wild veldt, and while quietly puffing and blowing a cloud of fragrant smoke, which he complacently watched curling to the roof, he began a review of things in general as they affected him particularly. Everything had not gone on quite smoothly during his absence. The garden had been neglected and become a wilderness. The Hall had been allowed to suffer; for instance, the rain had come through the roof; and through the want of fires the walls and pictures had been injured. Rats had infested the place, and worse still, burglars had effected an entrance, after poisoning his favourite house dog, and had got off with a large portion of the family plate.

The old man and his wife were quite useless; and he felt that he himself must look after the safety of his house and property. Plumbers must be employed to attend to the drains, which had got out of repair; builders must be engaged to repair the roof of the hall; and gardeners set to work to put the garden, in which the squire took great interest, right. More servants were wanted, and, in short, a host of minor, but necessary matters must be put into shape. As he smoked, this is the form his thoughts took:

"Well, it is a dreary, worrying outlook.... Nothing but expense and trouble ... and all for one solitary man, who could do without it all if necessary. . . ." And here, the advice of Mrs. Graves recurred to him. "Should he take it? . . . Would it be wise to do so? Should he marry and settle down like an ordinary Philistine? Such a thing was within the bounds of possibility . . . but, by Jove, I don't intend to be hurried, let alone rushed into it! . . . After all, I am romantic enough to refuse to marry without love, and, at present, my heart is quite my own. Marriage is a large order; and a man is an egregious ass who enters on it lightly. . . . I know that the course of true love never did run smooth; and I'll avoid all the worry and trouble attending it as long as I can. . . . Still, if I really loved a woman, I should be willing to encounter difficulties and dangers to secure the object of my passion These well-meaning idiots want to make it too easy for me; but I am not quite such a fool as to fall into a pit dug for me under my very nose."

Thus the squire soliloquised before the fire in the breakfast room, and, later, he walked over part of his estate, occasionally stopping for a chat with one of his tenants, and talking over necessary repairs and improvements.

Workmen were called in and had to be looked after. In time, this began to prove monotonous, and Carruthers began to think of some other way of passing the day. He did not care to see too much of his neighbours, and although the old Hall possessed a fine library of choice books, he could not read all day. Then it suddenly struck him that he had received an invitation to visit his old college chum, Vincent Cholmondeley and his wife at their home, the Grange. He at once made up his mind to start tomorrow and make a day of it. The next day was Sunday; that would suit him as well as any other. He knew the country round about well and had often walked there in his boyish days, although it was a good distance off. Since he had been away, however, a new line of railway had been finished which would take him to within ten minutes' walk of his friend's place, and he thought he would use it. He accordingly took a return ticket to Slowboro, the village near the Grange, and left by the morning train. These rural trains did not run frequently, but he managed to reach his destination by one o'clock. He made sure that Vincent and his wife would already be at luncheon, and that he would join them. He sauntered leisurely from the station, and soon found himself before the gates of the Grange. He rang the bell, whereupon the porter's wife issued from the lodge and opened the park gates. She was an elderly woman, hale and well preserved. As she admitted Carruthers, he noticed that she looked very hard at him as she dropped a curtsey. Where had he seen her before? On inquiry whether his friends were at home, he received a negative answer. They were still on the Continent, she said, and it was uncertain when they would return.

She did not know where they were; but letters were to be forwarded to the Paste Restante, Paris.

"Would the gentleman like to go in and leave a letter?" the woman inquired.

"Well, my good woman, that is just what I should like to do. I am an old friend of Mr. Cholmondeley, and should like to look over the house."

"I am sure you are quite welcome to do so, Sir Ashleigh," she said with a curtsey.

"You seem to know my name," remarked the squire. "Your face, too, seems familiar to me."

"Oh, I know you very well, Sir Ashleigh; though I can't expect you to remember me! My maiden name was Sarah Parsons. I was employed in your father's house as nurse to you, sir, when you were quite a little boy."

"What! You are Nurse Sarah!" exclaimed Carruthers. "Why, of course; I remember you now. I felt sure that I had seen you somewhere."

"Yes, Sir Ashleigh, I married Mathews, your father's head gardener, and we set up for ourselves and reared a large family of children. Most of them are in service. My eldest boy went out to South Africa and wrote home that he is in the same regiment as Captain Carruthers."

"What, your son, Private Mathews! I know him well. How strange! We will talk over this another time."

"As you please, Sir Ashleigh. Will you step into the house and take a little snack and a glass of home-brewed ale?"

"Well, nurse, I think I will accept your kind offer," he answered.

Captain Carruthers walked on to the house, entered first one room and then another, and finally seated himself at an escritoire in the drawing-room and penned a brief letter to his friend, which he left on the blotter just as Mrs. Mathews was returning from preparing a little lunch for him in the breakfast-room. As she was leaving him there, Carruthers called her:

"Stay, nurse, don't run away, but sit down and tell me all the family news you can, whilst I appease my hunger."

Thus encouraged, she seated herself and unlimbered her tongue, giving her guest many an anecdote of his early life—of course, with the most elaborate detail.

• • •

CHAPTER IV
PHYLLIS BROWN

◯

arruthers remembered some of the anecdotes which told against himself, and laughed heartily when his old nurse retailed some of these pranks of his youth. Mrs. Mathews made inquiries about her son, and was delighted when the Captain informed her that the young fellow was alive and well, and was by that time on his way home. The fond mother favoured Carruthers with a long account of her boy's illnesses, "all along of that waxination business," and other particulars to which he listened with exemplary patience. She also advised the captain, "when he did think of entering the marriage state, which she hoped would not be long first, never to have none of his children waxinated."

By this time the captain had finished his light luncheon, and expressed his readiness to be conducted over the house and grounds.

While they passed from room to room Mrs. Mathews did not spare her companion a single legend or story concerning the house and family, to which he made a show of listening. After some hours had passed, Sir Ashleigh looked at his watch, and informed his guide that he had some friends residing in the adjacent town of Abbotswood, and that, finding himself so near, he thought he would call on them. He pressed a sovereign in the old nurse's hand, and was hastening away before she had nearly finished her thanks.

"If you'll take my advice, Sir Ashleigh, you won't attempt to walk to Abbotswood on foot. You'll not be able to reach it before nightfall, and—and—"

"And what, my good woman?" he asked.

Here Mrs. Mathews beckoned to him to return, and stepped towards him herself.

"It's not safe to be out late o' nights for everybody," she said mysteriously.

"Why, nurse, do you still want to treat me like a baby? What is there to be afraid of? Are there robbers about?"

"Worse than that, it may be! There be strange tales in these parts—"

"A fig for tales!" said the Captain, snapping his fingers. "What are they about? Turnip-headed ghosts, I suppose. Well, nurse, I never knew that you were superstitious before. We'll have a good talk on the subject some other time. Goodbye! I don't want to be later than I can help, and a good walk will do me good!"

"I know you of old, Sir Ashleigh, for a wilful man, and a wilful man must e'en have his own way, but don't forget as I warned you!" shouted the old servant, as the Captain hurried his departure. Carruthers only waved his hand, for the clack, clack, clack of the old woman's interminable tongue was getting on his nerves.

Nurse Mathews gazed after him, shook her head, and returned to the lodge.

"What on earth does the well-meaning old idiot mean by her warning?" thought Carruthers. "That's what comes from being a peasant; and I now remember she hails from Lancashire, and the superstition of the people there is proverbial. Who has not heard of the Lancashire witches and their absurd doings? Yes, that accounts for it. These peasants are all alike."

Now Carruthers, like all men of healthy and well-balanced mind, was not prone to superstition; but on the other hand, he was not such an obstinate sceptic as to persistently deny, without an attempt at investigation, certain mysteries which have been hastily and ignorantly styled supernatural. For him the supernatural did not exist. Everything was natural—even a ghost!

"What! a ghost natural!" exclaims the reader. Certainly, my friend. And here I am not referring to any vulgar case of mere imposture, but to the real bona-fide old-fashioned ghost, believed in by our ancestors, who were not quite such idiots as some superficial, flippant persons of today find it pleasant to imagine.

"How do you make that out?" a sceptical reader inquires.

"I thought that modern education had banished once and for all these superstitions of our ignorant ancestors, and rightly consigned them to the limbo of the past." Not so fast, my dear sir; your modern education had apparently advanced you very little. I freely admit it has given you more conceit, made you a greater prig than you were before; but that is all. I do not wish here to enter upon a dissertation about the occult in nature, as there are many books upon the subject, and any of my readers who are honestly and intelligently interested in the question may, by studying them, discover the *raison d'être* of those strange phenomena for themselves; and, perhaps the gratifying result will be that they will think more and talk less on a difficult and profoundly interesting subject.

Carruthers, as we said before, was not an unreasoning sceptic in reference to things occult, when he had them on the best authority, and when they would bear investigation; but he was deaf on principle to silly village gossip because it was without reliable proof and authority. The warning words of his old nurse passed by him like the wind.

The day was unusually fine, the sky clear and bright, the air balmy and caressing; and, being sensitive to outward influences, he felt in high spirits and in no humour to indulge in gloomy anticipations.

He walked on with a buoyant step, eagerly drinking in the beauties of nature, as if they were part of himself as, indeed, they were.

The distant corn-fields, the pale blue hills beyond, with their enveloping haze, appeared to melt into the sky, while the russet slopes and valleys of the middle distance, the fine elms and other trees nearer the foreground, all of which he had known, admired, and loved from a boy, were all fraught with some sad and tender associations.

He recalled the time when he was a lad of about fourteen and had a boyish attachment to one Phyllis Brown, a girl about his own age, the daughter of a woodcutter, who lived in the most picturesque cottage he ever remembered to have seen. He had not yet reached it; but there, yes, there was the green lane where they were wont to meet; and a little way further on was the very seat where they had so often watched the glories of sunset and had kissed and looked into each other's eyes as if heaven itself was only there. Oh, the innocence and purity of those early attachments!

How near to heaven are our souls in those sublime moments! "How silly! How ridiculous" sneers the cynical man of the world.

"How decidedly improper!" ejaculates some grim spinster who has never risen above the lowest Sunday School plane.

"They both deserve to be soundly whipped and sent to bed fasting!"

Many things had happened to Carruthers since the days of his youth which were calculated to wipe out all memory of that innocent, and therefore, happy time; but now, under some strange influence, perhaps sent to save him from coming danger, all came back to him clearly and distinctly.

He murmured to himself:

"Pretty, tender-hearted little Phyllis! How he loved her, and how she loved him" Where was she now? Perhaps gone to service, poor little rosebud! Maybe she is married to some bumpkin of her own class, and has now grown coarse and material, with a large family of brats at her heels. Should I ever see her again? Her cottage home cannot be far off now. Why, good heavens, surely that is the spot, and, eh, what? No! As I live they have pulled down the cottage and built, oh horror! a brand new public house on its site."

This was too much for the romantic nature of our hero. He stood stock-still with his indignant eyes fixed on the desecrated spot.

At length, with a deep sigh and slackened pace, he approached the gaudy building, which was closed, the day being Sunday. A commonplace looking man, in his Sunday clothes, was leaning against a lamp-post smoking.

This worthy, whom Carruthers rightly guessed to be the landlord, looked up as he passed, and the captain spoke to him.

"You are the landlord of this tavern, I suppose?"

"At your service, sir," was the answer.

"Perhaps you can tell me how long this inn has been built?"

"Aye, that I can sir," answered the man. "It's getting on for eleven years come Michaelmas, as I built it myself, in place of the old, rubbishy cottage as I bought of a woodcutter, named Brown."

"You know Brown, then?" inquired Carruthers.

"Aye, sir, he was a man with a large family, all since growed up and gone out to service."

"Did you say all of them?" inquired the captain.

"Well, sir, let me think a bit. Yes, nearly all of them; except one as died—a girl about sixteen, called Phyllis—and a prettier, sweeter lass you couldn't meet in a day's march."

"Poor girl!" murmured the captain, and before he spoke again he had to master his emotion. "What was the cause of her death?"

"Why, sir, some said it was consumption; others—"

"Yes, the others, what did they say?" demanded Carruthers.

"Well, sir, I don't give credit to all the gossip of the countryside; but many people do say that the poor, pretty lass died pining for the love of a handsome young squire."

"Ah!" exclaimed Carruthers, with painfully assumed indifference; though he was obliged to turn his back on the man for a short time, gaze at the sky, and then look at his watch.

"Yes, sir, I expect we shall get it a bit later on—the rain and thunder, I mean. It has been very 'ot all day," said the man in reference to the captain's study of the rapidly gathering rain clouds.

"Yes, I think you are right," said Carruthers. Presently he went on: "And the father—Brown, I think you said that was his name—what became of him?"

"He was terrible cut up at the death of his favourite daughter, was the old man. He said as how it was witchcraft; but Lord, sir, the country folks about 'ere be that superstitious—there, it beats all, it does," said the enlightened publican.

"I know it," our hero answered. "It is so in all country places; but I imagine that a great deal of it is dying out now."

"Well, I don't know, sir; it may be in some places, but not about 'ere. Why, sir, they actually believes about 'ere in vampyres as disguises themselves in a beautiful form and sucks the blood of innocent babes and kills 'em! There, sir, such ignorance as that beats me, it do!"

"Ah, well, superstition is very hard to die!" said the captain; "but tell me," he added, "what became of the old man, Brown?"

"Oh, yes; beg pardon for not answering you before! Why, he married again and went to Australia; and no one never 'eard of him no more."

"Thanks for your information. It is very interesting. I have been in these parts before, and remember the little cottage. Tell me, how far is it to Abbotswood?"

"A good fifteen miles; but it's not easy to get there 'cross country after dark, 'less you knows the roads like your own pocket."

"Oh, I know the road well enough, thank you; good day!"

And Carruthers walked off hurriedly, glad to be alone with his thoughts and memories and able to brood over his emotions without interruption.

•••

CHAPTER V
A STRANGE MEETING

"**P**oor little Phyllis!" muttered Carruthers, as he walked on with quickened step, while the sun sank slowly in the west and gave every promise of a splendid but stormy sunset. "Poor girl, poor girl! And that was to be the end of our early love! . . . Perhaps better so. I could not have endured to see her develop into a coarse, vulgar woman, united to some drunken drudge of a husband, with a lot of untidy children at her heels. . . . Well, well, rest her soul, poor girl! But to say that she died through pining for love of me is, at the least, doubtful. . . . . Dying for love only occurs in story books. . . . I should like, however, to know the truth. . . . It was probably consumption brought about by a neglected cold; but as to witchcraft having anything to do with it, that, I think, is too absurd to believe. . . . It is surprising how ready the rustic mind is to put everything down to the supernatural that baffles its understanding."

Thus Carruthers mused as he strode on in the now fast-deepening twilight, stopping at intervals as he watched the great orb of day descend below the horizon in flaming colours of gold and purple! "How grand! How gorgeous a spectacle!" he muttered, as he stood rooted to the spot with his greedy eyes fixed on the afterglow. What noble thoughts did it call forth? What sublime, unspeakable feelings stirred within him? Soon the radiant colours faded into a uniform grey, enveloping the brilliant scene in hues of sombre sadness.

Soft memories of Phyllis would arise in his heart, and the scene before him appeared to harmonise with his melancholy feelings.

But being a robust, healthy man, he shook off this unusual mood, comforting himself with the following sophistry: "Bah! she was but a child! We were both children. . . . It was, after all, only boy and girl play. . . . Had she lived what could she have been to me? Besides, I had forgotten her."

Carruthers had been walking for some time now, and the darkness had gradually risen from the earth, like a series of gauze veils, and only a few stars were visible. The sound of a distant church bell reminded him it was Sunday, and, a few miles further on, the lights from a church window stood out from the surrounding shadows. This, he thought, could be no other than the very ancient church of St. Cuthbert, that had been built on the ruins of some heathen temple in the early dawn of Christianity. Carruthers knew it well, and indeed, had often strolled through the churchyard with Phyllis in his boyhood, trying to decipher the epitaphs of the old, moss-covered tombstones. He remembered a gigantic yew tree with its gnarled, widely spreading, serpent-like roots that tradition said was standing before the present church was built. Its age was even estimated to be sixteen hundred years. Would it be there now? And the old vicar whom he had known, would he still be in the land of the living?

A mist was now rising which, together with the deepening twilight, obscured his path, but he groped his way along until his foot encountered an obstacle. Stretching forth his hand he discovered that it was the low stone wall which enclosed the churchyard. He knew now that he was only about a mile distant from Abbotswood. The church bell had stopped, but the light through the stained-glass windows reached him through the trees. His walk had been a long one, and he felt that he needed a rest. He resolved to enter the church, and vaulted over the low wall, and, in doing so, almost fell into an open grave on the other side, but he dexterously avoided this unpleasant experience, and entered the edifice by a side door. The congregation, he observed, was exceedingly meagre. He sat down in one of the seats near the door, and looked around. Yes, there was the old man whom he had last seen hale and hearty, but who was now old and decrepit. The vicar gave out the hymn which precedes the sermon. A hymn-book lay before him, and he was busying himself in finding the one to be sung, when, looking up for an instant, he perceived that he was not alone in the pew. A lady, dressed in deep mourning, apparently a widow, tall, graceful, and youthful, had entered unseen, while he was turning over the pages of the book. Seeing that she was without one he offered to share his with her; and took the opportunity to scan her features, which struck him as romantically beautiful, though her skin was of an almost ghostly pallor, from which her rather deeply set black and flashing eyes stood out in the boldest relief. Her hair was of a purple blackness; her lips full, brilliantly red and prominent; the shape, however, was that of a perfect Cupid's bow. She had taken off one glove from the hand with which she held the hymn-book, and the Captain noticed, with keen eyes, that it was small and delicately shaped, but that the fingers were rather too pointed at the tips, and the nails, although filbert-shaped, grew over them and assumed the appearance of claws. This peculiarity he had before noticed in consumptive people; but not to so great a degree. He rapidly summed up the lady to be a young widow still mourning for the death of her dearly loved husband, and who was, partly through grid on the verge of consumption.

The warm sympathy of the soldier was aroused for her. He felt drawn to her by a mysterious power. It was a compound feeling, partly love and partly sympathy; but it was, at least, a strong feeling of interest, in addition to the pity and admiration which she had aroused.

"So young and so unfortunate and unhappy!" he said to himself as his glance rested oftener on her pale, romantic beauty than on the printed page.

He noticed that her voice did not join in the singing, and when the hymn was finished she mutely thanked him with a smile, and slight inclination of her head, raising her deep, flashing eyes momentarily at the same time.

What deep magnetic power was there in that brief, almost furtive glance, that caused his heart and nerves to thrill and throb as neither had ever done before?—It was a mixture of keen delight and keener pain.

He must find out who she was. He would not let her pass away out of his life.

No; he would follow her, if necessary, to the ends of the earth rather than that. As this thought and resolution flashed through brain and heart, the venerable vicar had ascended the pulpit, and soon gave his text, which happened to be from Ezekiel, chapter xxxvii, and part of the twelfth verse: "I will open your graves and cause you to come up out of your graves."

It struck Carruthers as an unusual one, and he wondered what the vicar would make of it in his sermon.

The vicar repeated the strangely weird text, and then he slowly examined the thin congregation. His eye soon alighted on the Lady in Black seated near Carruthers, and at once fixed there in a stony stare. The colour left his face, his eyes appeared to almost start from their sockets, his jaw dropped, and with a wild exclamation, he fell senseless to the bottom of his pulpit. There was an immediate stir amongst the worshippers, and the verger, who, fortunately, was a very tall, powerful man, hurried up the pulpit stairs, and carried the spare, thin form of the vicar down the steps, through the church, into the vestry.

A storm had been gathering its forces since sunset, and now, ripe for destruction, burst in all its fury. Vivid flashes tore the dark, heavy clouds in quick succession, and the detonations of thunder claps which followed each other at quicker and quicker intervals caused the old church to shake to its foundations, and, indeed, appeared to threaten to bury the congregation, already pale with terror, under its crumbling ruins. They hesitated whether to brave the storm and rush for home or to wait for the fury of the storm to lessen. The lightning did abate, in time, and the people left the church. When Carruthers looked around for his companion, to his utter astonishment, she had disappeared.

• • •

CHAPTER VI

THE TEMPTRESS

◯

When Ashleigh Carruthers found himself deserted by his companion, he, without a moment's delay, instinctively started in pursuit of her. Uncovered by an umbrella, he braved the pelting rain, and rushing down a sloping pathway which led to the high road to Abbotswood, he ran on inspired by the hope of overtaking the woman who had so strangely bewitched him. The rain came down with increased violence; and, after a time, he looked round for a temporary place of shelter. At last he reached a sort of small natural alcove, rather shallow, and covered with brambles, which grew on a rocky bank above. He entered the place, and, at first, thought he was alone. Presently, however, he heard the rustle of a woman's dress. He turned suddenly to learn who was so near him; and, in doing so, touched the shoulder of his companion. The lightning was nearly over, but at this moment a most vivid flash made everything in the place visible, and revealed to him the features of the woman for whom he was searching.

"I beg your pardon; I thought I was alone in this strange place of shelter," apologised the Captain, whose eyes had lighted up with pleasure.

"Oh, indeed, there is no occasion for apology! What dreadful weather, is it not?" She uttered the words in the most amiable tone of voice.

"Yes," replied Ashleigh, "I have travelled a good deal, but this is as bad as almost anything I have experienced."

"You have travelled, then?" said the lady. "I observed your dress and bronzed face, and imagined you had just returned from South Africa. No doubt, you have been in action."

"Yes, I have been in several; in fact, I was in the war from the very beginning."

"What a beautiful sight a battlefield must be!" she said.

"Beautiful!" exclaimed the Captain in astonishment, "nay, madam, it is horrible in the extreme; and no sight for you, I am sure."

When a lady from whom he expected delicate and refined thoughts and feelings callously expressed a distinct admiration for the horrors of a battlefield, Carruthers felt unfavourably impressed, and had it not been for the effect produced by her strange attractions, he would have been revolted.

By this time the rain had ceased, and the rapidly drifting clouds revealed the moon and stars shining above them.

"I think it is sufficiently fine now to permit us to quit our shelter," he said. "May I ask where you are going?"

"To Abbotswood," she answered.

"So am I," he said. "May I accompany you?"

"With pleasure," she replied. "You have friends there, I presume?"

"I have, but shall not disturb them tonight. I intend to put up at the Abbot's Hotel," he said.

"I intend going there myself," said the lady. "I have no friends in the town, in fact, I am quite alone in the world."

"Indeed, I am very surprised; one would imagine a lady of your attractions would have many friends. Is your home in this district?" inquired Carruthers.

"I have no fixed dwelling place. I roam the world at my own caprice, remaining in any place as long as it pleases me, and when I am tired of it, trying another," she said.

Carruthers perceived that he had met with a character, a woman of independent will; perhaps, a "new woman." He had heard of the genus, but had not as yet met with a specimen; and was not prepared to admire when one presented herself. Carruthers' idea of excellence in woman was sweetness and tenderness; in short, femininity.

A man generally likes a woman whose qualities are the opposite of his own; and, on the other hand, it is certain that a woman does not care for an effeminate man.

After a pause, Carruthers inquired whether she enjoyed her solitary life.

"As much as it is possible for me to enjoy anything," she replied.

"You have never, then, felt the want of a companion—some one to share existence with you?" inquired the Captain.

"That is according to circumstances," she said.

"If you want to learn whether I should like to be indissolubly linked to a man whom I might afterwards learn to dislike and despise, then most decidedly not; I love my freedom too much. Companionship is agreeable until it palls. When that occurs people are better apart."

If Carruthers had felt anything approaching a serious attachment for this strange and fascinating creature, the plain avowal of such principles would have checked the feeling. Might not such a woman soon tire of him, and, in time, learn to despise him?

No, no, such originality and independence did not please Carruthers!

These were, indeed, unconventional ideas; but he was not sufficiently weaned from the general opinion which had prevailed in the past to accept such a new order of things. He had sufficient worldly tact, however, not to enter into a discussion in a case where they differed so deeply and widely, and changed the subject of conversation by remarking:

"By the way, and it is strange that I have not alluded to it before, I wonder what it was that so affected the vicar as to cause him to faint after giving out the strange text he selected?"

"I should imagine that he is subject to such attacks," suggested the lady in the iciest tones and without a touch of sympathy.

As her companion keenly scrutinised her countenance, which, lit up by the cloudless moon, appeared hard and set, and there were cruel lines about the mouth, in spite of her prominent, full, red lips. It might arise from her manner, but to Carruthers there seemed to be a very marked want of sympathy and womanly softness in her, which were the very qualities he most admired and appreciated in the opposite sex. He could not understand her; and, therefore, thought he would pursue the conversation in order to make an attempt to do so.

"Do you know," he said, "it struck me that the vicar fixed his eyes on you with, strange to say, when you are concerned, a look of horror; and then immediately fell senseless on the floor of his pulpit!"

"Ah, you observed that did you?" she said indifferently.

"Yes, it appeared to me that he had seen you before, and under very unpleasant circumstances; in fact, if I may say so, he appeared to dread, and hate you."

"He does hate me," she replied curtly and coldly.

"Then I was right in my supposition?" said Carruthers; "but how is it possible—" He was about to add, "that one so young, fascinating, and beautiful, could inspire a feeling of hatred?"

The reason he did not complete the sentence was that he, at the moment, noticed the cold, hard, merciless look in the countenance, now lighted up by the full moon, and he instinctively felt that such a poor attempt at a small compliment must fall flat on a nature so cold and unimpressionable, and refrained.

"Oh, it's a long story, and not very amusing," she broke in; and stopped, for a bat flitted about her head as she began to speak, and appeared to want to settle there, but she brushed it away with the hand several times; and, in the action, exposed one of her ears, which though small and beautifully shaped on the whole, Carruthers observed to have a pointed top. At the same time she smiled; not a hearty, sweet, lovable smile; but a weary, melancholy, and sarcastic one. The Captain was then, for the first time, able to notice her teeth, which, though white and well-shaped, had the canine form rather more developed than is strictly in accordance with beauty.

In spite of these defects, which his keen eyes detected, he felt himself drawn to her in an unaccountable manner; in spite of all his criticisms. She had but to fix her large, lustrous black eyes full upon him to make him her abject slave.

"How beautiful you are!" he exclaimed, in a burst of enthusiastic admiration which appeared to carry him away.

She smiled on him with gratified vanity, and her humid eyes flashed with passion.

"Beautiful creature!—may I?—can I?—dare I? Ah!" and Carruthers wild with admiration, threw open his arms, and in an instant they were clasped tightly round the slim waist of the woman, while his lips were pressed vehemently against her prominent red mouth, as if nothing on earth could ever separate them.

Oh, the rapture of that long, voluptuous embrace! How the fierce heart's blood ran riot in his veins, as his manly, nervous arms encircled that fair form with frantic clasp, and held her to his throbbing heart, his lips still glued to hers! Here beneath the silvery light of the moon the lovers stood entwined in each other's arms, oblivious of the whole world in the delirium of their passion. Close to them was a rustic bench which was placed between two huge trees, the thickness of the interlaced branches above forming such a protection from rain as to have left the seat dry, in spite of the fury of the late storm. Here they both seated themselves. They were now not far from the town, yet no one was astir. Not a sound disturbed the silence of the night. Again, and again, they kissed and caressed each other until he, at last, struggled to release himself in order to breathe more freely, for he felt almost stifled. As he momentarily liberated himself from her grasp, he noticed, for the first time, the odour of her breath, which was like a charnel house. Yet, such was the overwhelming intensity of his passion, that he heeded it not, neither did it repel him; in fact, as far as its effect on him went, it might have been the proverbial perfume of Arabia. So thoroughly was he under the spell of her magnetism that he had also forgotten the repugnance aroused by her canine teeth, her pointed ears, and clawlike finger tips. To him, in his infatuation, everything about her was perfection, and he would have fought to the death with anyone who had dared to disparage her charms. He had found the right woman at last, he told himself. As they reclined, locked in each other's arms in the very tumult of their passion, a dizziness came over Carruthers, accompanied by a wild singing in his ears. Then a voice that appeared to come from far away, and gradually assumed greater and greater distinctness, as it sang through his brain, called him by his name.

Ah, how well he remembered the sweet musical tones of that voice! No; he could not be mistaken!"

"Ashleigh! dear Ashleigh!" it cried in agonised tones, "Come away ere it is too late! Oh, beware, you are ensnared by a demon from hell! It is I, Phyllis, who warns you! I, too, was her victim!" Then the same voice uttered a wail of agony; died away, and was heard no more. At this moment a bat fluttered about their heads. The ardour of the two abated, and Carruthers recovered enough sense to remember that the hour was late, and the hotel might be closed if they delayed longer, so he suggested to his enchantress, whose name he had not thought of asking, that they should wend their steps towards the town.

They both rose from the wooden bench, and wandered for a time across the common with their arms around each other's waists. But what was the feeling that had come over Carruthers? He actually felt more tired and exhausted than when he at first sat down to rest after his long walk. He seemed strangely depleted of vital force. His head swam, his limbs had lost their elasticity, and his steps dragged heavily. His companion on the contrary seemed to have gained new vitality; she laughed and joked, now and again leaving his side, and skipping gaily in front of him in the exuberance of her spirits, and saying in a tone in which might be detected some mockery: "Let us see, dearest, which of the two will arrive first!"

Carruthers looked after her, amused by her banter and high spirits, when lo, to his unmeasured astonishment, she had vanished from his sight as if dissolved in air!

Rooted to the earth with amazement at her mysterious disappearance, for some considerable time, his first impulse was to run in pursuit; but the wide common, the whole expanse of which was in the light of the moon as clear to his eye as in broad day, afforded no trace of her.

• • •

CHAPTER VII
IN DANGER OF DEATH

◯

O ur hero was dazed and bewildered by the mysterious disappearance of his late companion. He did not, however, jump to the conclusion that there was anything supernatural in it. On the contrary, she had been to him a real flesh and blood woman, especially when she had so passionately pressed her red, pouting lips to his. Nothing could have been more warm and substantial. Then he remembered what in the height of excitement he had ignored—the bad odour of her breath. When he thought of it, he wondered how he could, even in his delirium, have overlooked it.

Being no longer under the powerful magnetic influence, which appeared to sweep all away in a torrent of passion, he was able to analyse his emotions and that brought about a change in his feelings to the woman.

He remembered that she had offered no resistance whatever to his first warm caresses as any ordinary woman would have done, if only for the sake of appearances, and to enhance the value of her surrender. Was he, who had so easily penetrated the wiles and arts of so many of the fair sex, to succumb at once to the mysterious creature whom chance had so strangely thrown in his way, and about whose position, name, and past he knew absolutely nothing?

In Carruthers' position, love, to be happy and secure, must end in marriage. He could not jeopardise his name and standing by loose attachments. Could he offer such a strange creature, who yielded at the first attack from a man she had only just met, marriage? Could he make such a woman, one who laughed and sneered at the solemn tie which had united the sexes for centuries, the mistress of Tudor Hall, and the mother of his children? No, no, no! Perish the thought! Were she ten times more beautiful he would not yield to her seduction.

And Carruthers began to recall the canine teeth, the pointed ears, the claw-like fingers, as well as the hard, stony cruelty of her expression, and her total want of human sympathy and womanly tenderness.

As he called all this up in his mind, he logically summed up against her, and put her down as a mysterious being destitute of heart, and of any human feeling of her kind. Passion of the lowest kind appeared to be her sole attribute. What a pity it seemed when he remembered her delicate, graceful form, and the exquisite beauty of her face and features.

As Carruthers pondered more deeply on his strange encounter, he was compelled to admit to himself that what he had felt for her, while his madness lasted, had not been love—no, a thousand times, no!— but mere wild, blind passion, inspired and sustained by her sheer will power! She had magnetised or hypnotised him, whichever term the reader may prefer; and it is only fair to admit that Carruthers was rather a good subject to be influenced in that manner by such a woman. Our ancestors and the peasantry of today would have made use of the word "bewitched" to describe the power she had so unscrupulously wielded.

As the captain thought over the whole adventure he said inwardly: "What's in a name? Is there, after all, much difference between the learned and the ignorant in regard to such a subject? Do not they both believe the same thing, though they may express their meaning differently? . . . Witchcraft! Did such a power exist? If not, how account for the manner in which he had been lately duped? How could he who rather prided himself in being a sensible, level-headed man, have allowed himself to be so easily duped; yes, duped, like an idiot! . . . Yes, he had allowed a stronger will than his own to dominate and degrade him! He had been taken unawares at his weak point, and had evidently not been quite 'all there' at the time. Perhaps his long walk had lowered his vitality and his nerves had been out of order."

Thus mused Carruthers; and the more he mused the more he hated himself for his egregious stupidity and loathed the woman.

The light mockery of her tones and words at parting galled him. Was the woman really a witch endowed with the mysterious power of appearing and disappearing at will; or was she only an agile trickster who had cunningly concealed herself behind some furze bush or hollow for fun? If so, he would be even with her, and let the joke fall flat by ignoring it.

With these thoughts animating him Carruthers strode on towards the town, without casting one look behind, and soon reached the Abbot's Hotel.

He walked in, ordered a bed, and, being very hungry, also supper. He made no inquiries as to whether a lady had reached the house before him, but took a seat in the coffee-room and awaited his meal.

All the hotel keeper could provide were pork chops, and these were rather underdone; but Carruthers was too hungry to criticise, and soon devoured them and drank a small bottle of claret. After which he filled his briar-root pipe and peacefully smoked until his nerves were a little quieter. He drank a glass of brandy and water about an hour later, and then retired to his room, tired in mind and body. He was soon between the sheets and snoring in the most unromantic and natural way imaginable.

Now, whether it was owing to the underdone pork chops, or to the brandy and water he had taken before retiring to rest, we cannot say; but the Captain had a most remarkable dream. He thought he was a boy again, and roaming the heather once more in order to keep tryst with his pretty Phyllis.

He had reached the seat at which they usually met, and from which her father's cottage could be seen. Yes, there it was, the little house with its thatched roof, lattice windows, and gable, its small garden, gay with hollyhocks and sweet peas, that he had so often admired.

Now, the door opened, and Phyllis ran out swiftly with a rustic hat on her pretty head, her sunny, beaming face and laughing, loving eyes looking as young and charming as ever. Soon they were in each other's arms, kissing and caressing, like two innocent children.

They sat on the seat close together holding each other's hands, while uttering those childish nothings which are so full of eloquence to love and innocence like theirs.

The sun was sinking in the west; they drew closer together and watched the glowing orb descend towards the distant horizon, when suddenly a dark cloud overspread the sky, from out of which blew a chilling blast, and, strange to say, the calm sweet face of the country was transformed into a dark, gloomy burial ground, filled with tombstones and monuments of various designs, interspersed with black yew and cypress trees.

Then a storm arose, accompanied with blinding lightning and terrible thunder. The graves burst open, and the dead in their white shrouds circled about and hovered in the air over their tombs; and, as they circled there, they appeared to be wailing and shrieking—yet, wonderful as it appears, no sound was to be heard! Then a huge bat with fiery eyes, that was perched on a tombstone, expanded its widely spreading black wings and flew fiercely towards them. Phyllis shrieked with terror and was lost to sight; but the demon bat attacked the youth and threw him down on his back. Fastening its terrible claws into his chest, and making an incision with its teeth, it proceeded to drain the young heart's blood, while at the same time fanning him into slumber and insensibility with its black wings.

The youth did his best to struggle against the hellish monster, but at last succumbed from sheer weakness.

The distant crowing of a cock was now heard, and Carruthers awoke. It must have been in the small hours of the morning, for the pale grey dawn was coming in at the windows. His brow was bathed in a profuse, cold perspiration, and when he tried to turn over to the other side he sank back exhausted by the effort. When he succeeded in raising himself on one arm his head began to swim. What was the matter with him, he wondered? The room appeared to whirl round and round, and he felt intoxicated. Carruthers made renewed efforts to rise; and, at length, by the means of almost superhuman will power and energy, succeeded in leaping from his bed. But no sooner had his feet touched the floor than he fell, and all efforts to rise were vain. He touched his chest, in which he felt pain, and encountered something wet and clammy. On examining it, he saw that it was blood. He grew alarmed. What could have happened to him? Perhaps an unimportant wound that he had received in action, and which had long since healed, had broken out again? But this seemed hardly possible. He crawled on his hands and knees to the washstand, and seizing a towel, tried to staunch the flow of blood. Then, making for the bell-rope in the same way, he pulled it with all the strength he could muster. After an interval the boots knocked at the door.

"Come in," said Carruthers in a faint voice.

On opening the door the man started in surprise and horror on seeing the hale and hearty man who had arrived at the hotel on the preceding night lying on the floor pale and with blood-stained shirt.

"Go—fetch a doctor—at once—quick! I think I am dying!" whispered the Captain.

The boots, now thoroughly aroused from his stupor, flew downstairs, and at his utmost speed ran for the nearest doctor.

• • •

CHAPTER VIII
THE BOOTS' STORY

◎

As the boots crossed the road in the direction of the doctor's house, he happened to meet that gentleman coming in the direction of the hotel.

He had just paid a visit to the Rev. Jabez Waldegrave, Vicar of St. Cuthbert's, who, the reader will remember, had fallen in a fit after delivering his text the previous evening.

His state had appeared to be dangerous, and Dr. Leach had been sent for. He had been with Mr. Waldegrave through the night and, thinking his condition improved, had left his patient and was on his way home when stopped by the boots.

"Please, sir, there's a gent at the inn lying helpless on the floor and bathed in blood," said the boots, in a breathless hurry.

"Why, what has happened?" inquired Dr. Leach.

"Don't know, I'm sure, sir. He says as he's dying. Arrived only last night, looking as strong as a 'ouse. Ordered a good supper, ate it 'earty like, had hot brandy and water, and turned in, sir. Early this morning 'is bell rang, and when I—"

"M'm—you say a gentleman, eh, boots?"

"Yes, sir, and that's the truth, he—"

"That will do. Show me to his room, at once," said the doctor quietly.

Dr. Leach, followed the boots up the creaking, old-fashioned staircase of dark oak with a curiously carved balustrade, and, on entering the room, found Carruthers lying prostrate on the floor, and looking terribly ill.

"Quick, bring me a bottle of your best brandy and a tumbler!" ordered the doctor. "Don't lose a moment!"

Without delay the boots obeyed the order. On his return, the doctor said: "Now, first assist me to raise this gentleman into a sitting posture. . . . So, that will do. Run and get me some ice as quickly as possible."

After administering a good dose of brandy, which brought a little colour into the ghastly face of his patient, the doctor asked him a few questions about his illness. Carruthers answered him with great difficulty.

The doctor's first impression was that his patient had attempted to commit suicide; but, on carefully examining the wound, he started with astonishment, and then asked with some eagerness how he accounted for the wound on his chest.

"I am unable to account for it, doctor. I have just returned from South Africa, where I was wounded in several places during action. This slight flesh wound on the chest soon healed, and I never thought it would break out again.

"Neither has it," answered Dr. Leach, looking at Carruthers suspiciously. "This wound was never a serious one, and healed up almost immediately; but the one you are now suffering from was savagely inflicted on the same spot, and what is stranger still, it bears the distinct impress of teeth." After a pause, he added impressively, "You must be aware of how it happened."

The doctor was extremely perplexed and annoyed at his patient's persisting in denying all knowledge of the facts.

"I declare to you, doctor," he said, "on my oath that all I know about the matter is this: I woke up last night, or, it may be, early this morning, and found my shirt covered with blood, and myself almost lifeless."

No further explanation could be obtained from him. Dr. Leach was unable to accept his patient's statement, even upon oath. He adhered to his opinion that the wound had been inflicted by teeth, and that it was perfectly impossible for Carruthers to be ignorant of the fact. If the print of the wound was really that of teeth, then, in his mind, it must have been inflicted by a woman out of spite or jealousy; and, evidently, the victim affected to deny all knowledge of the fact in order to screen her. It was evidently a delicate and difficult matter to probe. Young and vigorous men, in good position, whenever they fall into an ugly scrape that might reflect on their honour and social standing, arc naturally reticent.

On these grounds, the astute doctor adhered to his own opinion, and wisely said no more. When the boots entered with ice, Dr. Leach applied it to the wound, saw his patient comfortably into bed, ordered him to be supplied with beef-tea and brandy; and prepared to take his leave.

"I shall call tomorrow, Sir Ashleigh, just to see how you are; and, in the meantime, telegraph for a trained nurse on whom I can depend."

"You know my name, doctor," said Carruthers. "May I ask who informed you?"

"Well, the fact is that I had just left the Vicar of St. Cuthbert's when boots brought me here. Mr. Waldegrave informed me that you attended his church last evening; and that though he had not seen you for years, he recognised you from your likeness to your father, who was an intimate friend of his."

"I understand," said Carruthers. "Well, did he say anything else about me?"

"Only this. He expressed a very strong desire to see and speak with you before his death; for the poor, old gentleman, who was very poorly before, appears to be terribly shaken by the fit he had last night, and, to be candid, I don't think he is long for this world. Mr. Waldegrave wished me to tell you that he had something very important to communicate."

"I will call on the vicar as soon as you will permit me to go out," said Carruthers.

"You must make up your mind not to stir from the house for a week, at any rate," said the doctor as he left the room.

A telegram was despatched to Tudor Hall, informing the house-keeper that the owner had met with an accident which would detain him at Abbotswood for a week or two.

Dr. Leach left the room with the full determination of, if possible, getting to the bottom of the mystery of the wound, and with this inten-tion, questioned the landlord as to whether any strange lady had slept in the hotel last night.

To this demand the man replied in the negative; and turning to his wife, said: "Did you, Polly, see any lady enter the hotel last night?"

"No, Bill," was the reply. "I never saw any lady."

"But I did," broke in the boots, "leastways I see one agoing out this mornin'. She were a-comin' down the stairs and just leavin' the room as is opposite the captain's."

"Well, if boots distinctly saw a lady going out, it is evident she must have first got in," said the doctor, who was nothing if not logical.

The boots looked puzzled, and Dr. Leach went on:

"Come, now, are you quite positive that you did see a lady leaving the hotel?"

"Can't say as how I can exactly swear to it; and what gets over me is as when I tore down the stairs to fetch you, sir, I found the street door locked and bolted just as I left it last night," said the boots, whose limited brain was getting addled under the unusual weight it had to sustain.

"You must have been dreaming, boy," said the landlord.

"No, sir, I wasn't dreamin'," said the boots, "for I was just a-cleanin' of myself when I 'eard the captain's bell, and I was hurrying off to answer it, when I caught sight of a lady a-goin' downstairs."

"What was she like, Tom?" inquired Maggie, one of the servants. "Can't say as I looked much at her," replied boots. "I only seed as how she were dressed all in black like a widder. On 'er hearin' my step she looked up for a moment and I seed as she was very pale, and had shiny black eyes—big 'uns, too. Her lips was very red, and she seemed to be a-sucking 'em like as if she had just 'ad a very nice breakfast."

"Well I never," broke in Maggie, "if that don't sound like a pictur' of the lady in black as all the countryside be a-talking of!"

"The lady in black!" exclaimed the alert doctor. "Why, who is she?"

"Oh, lor, sir!" replied the ready-tongued Maggie, "the folks in these parts tells the queerest tales about a certain lady in black what none ever heered the name of or how, or where she lives. They say as she leaves death and destruction behind her wherever she goes."

"Tut, wench, rubbish!" interrupted the landlord. "Don't be offending the doctor's ears with all the rubbishin' tales the ignorant folks tells about here, but just run upstairs and see if that bedroom has been slept in."

Maggie rushed upstairs to obey her master's orders, and quickly returned with a scared look upon her fat face.

"Oh, lor, sir! the bed ain't even been slep' in, but there's some drops of blood on the passage leadin' from the Captain's room right across the landin' to the chamber opposite. The washstand basin 'as been used, too, and the water is mixed with blood, and there's blood stains on the towel."

"This looks like foul play," said the doctor, "and must be inquired into. I will go round immediately to the police station and place the matter in the inspector's hands."

Without further words, Dr. Leach left the hotel, and walked over to the police station.

• • •

CHAPTER IX
ENTER NURSE EVEREST

◯

Within half an hour Dr. Leach returned to the hotel, accompanied by the chief police constable and a detective.

They were taken upstairs to the room supposed to have been occupied by the mysterious lady in black, and found everything there in the condition described by Maggie. After making the strictest investigation, every detail of which was jotted down by the detective, the constable said that in order to expedite matters it would be necessary to question the victim of the strange attack.

Here the doctor explained that his patient was at present in a very weak condition, barely able to speak; and, on that ground, it would be advisable to defer the interview for a few days.

When the doctor had gone, the constable and detective saw the hotel proprietor, his wife and servants, and questioned them all closely. Snapshots were taken of the finger-marks on the towel; and later, footprints were discovered on the landing, where some dust had collected, showing the marks made by a lady's small boot. All possible particulars bearing upon the question were carefully noted. The boots and shoes of all the inmates of the hotel were demanded, and their dimensions carefully compared with the footprints visible in the dust on the landing; and all were seen to be decidedly different. Closer investigation revealed a small portion of delicate black lace that had been caught in the lock of the door and torn off; also one solitary black hair of unusual length was found on the dressing-table; but most important, perhaps, of all, a gold ring was picked up, which had originally been massive, although designed for a delicate lady's finger, but had been worn thin by time. This, it was imagined, had been dropped by the lady when wiping the blood stains from her hands on the towel.

The length, breadth, and height of the room were carefully measured and noted, and when every possible examination had been made and entered in the note-book, the men left the hotel.

That night a hospital nurse arrived at Abbotswood by the last train, and was conducted to the hotel by Dr. Leach, and introduced to the patient. It was a happy chance that brought Nurse Everest to take charge of the sick man. She was a bright, cheerful, intelligent, and good-looking young woman, and seemed to inspire confidence by her quiet, unobtrusive manner, natural tact, and pleasant voice. Sir Ashleigh Carruthers was evidently pleased with her, for as he watched her movements, all of which were animated by a desire to do her best without the suspicion of fussiness, a pleased smile animated his pale face. She was given the room lately occupied by the mysterious visitor, and entered without delay on the discharge of her duties.

The liking felt for her by Carruthers was instinctively returned, and so good was the influence she exercised on the patient, and so pleasant the little talks they had together, that when Dr. Leach called the next morning, he was surprised at the change for the better visible in his patient.

A few days later he was well enough to be interrogated by the chief constable, who asked permission to examine his wound. After doing so, he said that it was exactly like others he had seen before, and most of which had been inflicted on children or growing girls, but never on old people. He was very hopeful about the ultimate capture of the would-be assassin, but would not go into the question of the use he intended to make of the chain of evidence in his possession.

The constable at length took his departure, having been unable to extract further information from the sick man than that obtained by Dr. Leach.

After the constable had gone, Carruthers and the nurse were left alone, and the conversation soon fixed upon the subject of the extraordinary woman in black, her motives, and her weird personality.

"Do you know, Sir Ashleigh," said Nurse Everest, "that I take a special interest in your case, not only because you are a pleasant and considerate patient—and that is not always the case, I can assure you—but because there is a mystery about it that I cannot fathom and which excites my curiosity."

"As it does mine, nurse; would I could probe it to the bottom! Now, however, that it is in the hands of the police, it is possible that with the help of the clues in their hands—"

"Begging your pardon, Sir Ashleigh," broke in the nurse, "but I was about to say that the police will have their work cut out for them if they have to deal with a lady who can appear and disappear whenever she likes, passing through closed doors without the customary ceremony of opening them."

"You have evidently made good use of your ears, nurse, since you have been here. Doubtless you found the conversation downstairs instructive and interesting."

"You may laugh at me if you please, Sir Ashleigh. It is not only from the talk downstairs that I form my opinion; but, in addition, from my own experience before I heard a word of your mysterious case, that causes me to view it in the most serious light."

"What do you mean, nurse?"

"Oh, Sir Ashleigh!" said the nurse tearfully, "how shall I tell you? I have for some time desired to speak freely, but feared to alarm you. Why should I worry you about matters foreign to my business? We nurses are engaged to attend to our patients; not to bother them with mysteries which do not concern them."

Here Nurse Everest took out her handkerchief and silently gave way to her emotion. Hospital nurses are carefully trained to master their feelings, especially in the presence of their patients, and this strange outburst on her part caused Sir Ashleigh alarm; because he knew that she was a woman of powerful will and much self-control.

"Why, nurse, what can be the cause of this emotion? You are usually calm and self-possessed; and I feel sure there must be an adequate reason for this outburst. Tell me all, without disguise or fear." This was said with genuine sympathy and good feeling.

But at this moment, Nurse Everest's keen ear heard the sound of footsteps in the passage, which was followed by a knock at the door. She rose, opened it, and admitted Dr. Leach.

On entering, much to the annoyance of Sir Ashleigh, the doctor inquired:

"Well, nurse, how is our patient progressing?"

"Very satisfactorily, sir," replied the nurse.

"He takes his beef-tea and a little brandy regularly, according to orders?" asked the doctor.

"That is well," said Dr. Leach. He then felt his patient's pulse, looked at his tongue, and, after asking him a few questions, said:

"Sir Ashleigh, I have just left Mr. Waldegrave, and I regret to say that he is sinking fast. He has had another fit, and being perfectly aware that his end is near, he is most desirous of seeing you before he dies. You have now had nearly a week in bed and look so much better that I think you may promise to visit him tomorrow, say, about 12 o'clock. I believe he will last until tomorrow night; besides, the intense desire he has to see you will help to keep him alive."

"Very well, doctor, I will call on him tomorrow unless I am much worse," said Carruthers.

"I will be here before 12 o'clock to see how you are, and if all is well, we will go together. Good morning."

After Dr. Leach's departure, Nurse Everest left Carruthers to prepare his meal. When Carruthers was alone, he began to think over what the nurse had said before the doctor's inopportune visit. "What was she about to tell me? What could her experience have been, and how could it throw any light on mine?"

In the midst of these reflections, Nurse Everest returned carrying a basin of beef-tea and a few slices of toast.

When Carruthers had enjoyed his meal, and the nurse had arranged his pillows deftly, he said:

"Well, nurse, what were you going to tell me when we were interrupted by Dr. Leach?"

"Oh, Sir Ashleigh," she began, "I have hardly had one hour's rest since I have been here, and my nerves are quite unstrung! That is why I could not help giving way just now; a thing I have never done before in all my life." She paused for a few moments to calm herself, and then went on:

"Every night I have been troubled with the most hideous dreams it is possible for the wildest imagination to conceive. Oh, indeed, indeed, they are too horrible to bear!" Here Nurse Everest shuddered violently.

Carruthers was filled with warm sympathy for the poor girl; and said in the most soothing and persuasive manner: "Calm yourself: tell me all; it will ease your mind, I am sure."

The nurse looked in her patient's face, and when she saw its expression a slight blush suffered her cheek as she continued her story.

"Well, Sir Ashleigh, on the night of my arrival, and before I had spoken to any of the people in the hotel, I returned to my room opposite this one, and feeling tired after my journey I almost immediately fell into a sound sleep. Presently I heard, or thought I heard, for I can't say positively whether I was asleep or awake, somebody moving about my room as if eagerly in search of something, although I was quite positive that I had locked the only door; a thing I invariably do.... This suggested the idea to me that someone must have been concealed under my bed with dishonest purpose; although what they hoped to purloin from a poor hospital nurse was a puzzle to me.... The room was dark and I could see nothing; but it appeared from what I heard that somebody was crawling about on their hands and knees looking for something.... After some time had passed the person seemed to rise and stand erect, and I heard a deep sigh and a sound as if the forehead had been struck with a gesture of despair. I was feeling too weak and drowsy to call out "Who are you and what do you want?" I merely sank back on my pillow, fell asleep, and had the following wonderful dream. . . . I seemed to be in an immense cave, deep in the bowels of the earth. A livid light from somewhere made visible long pendant stalactites of strange, fantastic forms, while on the ground, heaped carelessly about, were great boulders and huge stones. At the mouth of the cave I saw a female figure standing. She turned her face in my direction and gazed fixedly. Oh, heavens, shall I ever forget that face! . . ." The nurse here paused for a few minutes to regain her self-possession. "That terrible countenance haunts me still! She was clad in black garments, and some people might call her physically handsome.

"But the character expressed on her features was deadly and cruel. Her pallor was the whiteness of death. Her hair was black as night. When I looked at her she was throwing up her arms with a wild despair, and exclaiming: 'Lost, lost! Oh, my lost soul! Alas, alas! the life of the body which was my all, and which I have maintained in all its human beauty throughout the centuries by wearing upon my finger my mystic ring with its magic and all-powerful hieroglyphics! Yes, that priceless, life-giving ring which I stole from the mummy of the Egyptian high priest of Heliopolis, Amen Anen, who was a great prophet under Amenhotep III. Oh, madness of despair, that ring is lost!—lost! And what is now left for me but to wither, to shrivel and die?'

"You can imagine the effect of this extraordinary speech upon me, Sir Ashleigh."

"I can, indeed, nurse, but pray, in heaven's name, go on!" he exclaimed impatiently.

"After some time spent in inarticulate wails, during which she beat her breast and tore her hair, the horrible creature continued:

"'The ring is lost which gave me immunity from old age, sickness, and all common ills that affect the vulgar herd of men and women. Yes, the loss of that charm is the loss of all. No longer can I continue to prolong my existence by draughts of human blood.

"'There is nothing before me now but horrible death and total extinction. Woe is me! I have no soul; I cannot pray! If I could the angelic powers might come down and help me!...I chose my fate. I had free will, and deliberately preferred the animal and sensuous life, spurning the higher claims of the spirit.... Yes, my ring has gone, and with it all life, all hope; I must die, die for ever!'

"Here I awakened; but since that night I have had the same dream, seen the same terrible, deathly looking creature, who ever calls out in despairing, desperate tones: 'Oh, that I had the wealth of the Indies to purchase back that slender band of mystic gold! My ring! My ring! Oh, give me back my ring!'"

• • •

CHAPTER X

CARRUTHERS AND NURSE EVEREST

○

"And did you really dream all that, nurse?" inquired Carruthers, "and on the night of your arrival, too?" After thinking deeply for some time, be added, "It is very remarkable, very wonderful, and appears to me to be less an ordinary dream than a vision, containing a spiritual premonition. Your clear recollection of it all is extraordinary. It must have made a deep impression on your mind to enable you to be so exact in every detail."

"True, Sir Ashleigh, and what is more the vision will not leave me in peace; it repeats itself every night; and there is hardly any difference in it."

"Depend upon it, nurse, that these visions are sent to you from heaven for some purpose. This is no ordinary case. We have had to deal with a vampire, there can be no reasonable doubt of that, strange as it may appear to our ordinary sense. Of course, I have read of such things in my youth, but never believed that they had any foundation in fact."

"Neither did I, Sir Ashleigh. Who would, or could, unless forced to do so by overwhelming evidence?"

"There is one thing I must say to you," said Carruthers, very earnestly, "I think it most important that we should keep all this to ourselves. I hate my private affairs to be the topic of outside talk. It will be sufficient for outsiders to know that a wound I received in action has reopened after unusual exertion, and that I am compelled to lay up for a time."

"You can depend on my silence being deep as the grave," the nurse said.

"I am quite sure of that, nurse; I place every confidence in you."

"If it should ever get into the papers it will not be through me, though how to keep it out altogether, now the police have a hand in it, I fear will be difficult," said Nurse Everest.

"I will enjoin them to keep it as dark as possible; but in the meanwhile I will not leave a stone unturned in my efforts to unearth the criminal. It will not be easy for her to escape the claws of the law now that she has lost her charm."

After a pause, which the nurse had the tact not to interrupt, during which Carruthers thought ruefully—"And I kissed her lips and made a perfect ass of myself. But who is proof against witchcraft?"—Nurse Everest said quietly: "Sir Ashleigh, if you don't require anything more, I should be glad to retire to rest, for I feel very tired and unstrung."

"Certainly, nurse, and I wish you good night and pleasant dreams." He shook hands with her, and they parted for the night.

• • •

CHAPTER XI

THE REV. JABEZ WALDEGRAVE'S STORY

D r. Leach called the next morning about ten o'clock. He found his patient already up and dressed and sufficiently well to pay the proposed visit to the vicar. The two set out together, Carruthers leaning on the doctor's arm and using a stick. He looked a good deal pulled down, but was manifestly on the high road to recovery. They reached the vicarage at a fortunate moment, when the sick man was enjoying an interval of comparative ease after being slightly delirious. Carruthers was shocked at the ghastly, death-like look of the vicar, who greeted him with evident pleasure: "I am glad you have come, Sir Ashleigh, at last," he said, in a faint whisper, to which his visitor had to bend his ear, "as I know perfectly well that my hours are numbered, and I should be loth to depart without doing my duty to the son of my old friend and benefactor—Sir Hugh Carruthers"—here he paused for a few minutes to regain sufficient strength to enable him to continue—"in whose company some of the happiest years of my life were spent. You are like him in appearance, and I should have known you anywhere . . . but to the point . . . my time is short. . . . I have some very important and extraordinary information to impart to you, and fearing lest my strength should fail before I could give it all to you *viva voce*, I have here a written account of everything it is necessary that you should know; it is signed by myself and duly attested . . . it is dated ten years ago. . . . There are, in addition, certain letters from members of my family and other documents, which will prove to you that I was perfectly sound in mind when the strange story was penned. . . . The facts therein contained, I admit, require all the confirmation attainable; in fact, the story is so far removed from the ordinary experience of humanity that anyone might be excused for skepticism, and even for doubting the sanity of the writer. . . . But I must not be prolix, though there is much more I should like to say." Here the speech of the rather garrulous old gentleman was broken by a violent fit of coughing, which made it impossible for him to go on.

Dr. Leach approached his patient, and taking his hand, said: "I think, Mr. Waldegrave, you have spoken enough for the present. Sir Ashleigh will doubtless find all you wish him to know contained in the manuscript. You had, I think," speaking to the vicar, "better take leave of him now, as it is my very sad duty to inform you that you have only a very short time to live."

Here the vicar extended his thin, nearly transparent hand to the son of his old friend, and with a kindly and satisfied smile as if he felt that an important duty had been discharged, sank back upon his pillow, and his eyes almost immediately became glazed.

The doctor watched closely, and said, "Poor old gentleman!—he's gone at last." He at once wrote out the death certificate and gave it to the woman in attendance.

Then, turning to Carruthers, he said, "Sir Ashleigh, now that our presence is no longer required here, I think I had better accompany you back to the hotel. You have had enough excitement and exercise for one day."

Carruthers placed the sealed MS in his big breast pocket, and with a last look at all that remained of his father's friend, the two left the house together. On their way Carruthers expressed great curiosity as to the nature of the strange disclosures the MS contained. There was a sphinx-like look in the doctor's face which gave him the impression that that gentleman knew more than he appeared willing to admit.

"It must be something very extraordinary; but, do you know, doctor, that I am prepared to believe anything now. You do not doubt the old gentleman's sanity, eh?"

"Of that there can be no possible question; neither of his uprightness and good faith—still——" and Dr. Leach pursed his lips.

"Here we are at the hotel entrance," said Carruthers. "I will not trouble you to come in; I can get upstairs without assistance."

"Well, then, Sir Ashleigh, if you are quite sure, I will say goodbye for the present, as I have another patient whom I ought to visit at once. Now, don't worry; feed well; and expect me tomorrow morning."

Carruthers waved his hand to the doctor, and ascending the stairs with the help of his stick, entered his room, of which Nurse Everest opened the door.

"So you're back again, Sir Ashleigh; and I hope not too tired."

"No, nurse, nothing to speak of."

After seating himself in his easy-chair and resting for a time, during which the nurse had the good sense to be quiet—what a blessed thing the full command of the tongue is!—Carruthers said:

"The old gentleman wanted to say a lot to me, but the exertion and excitement were too much for his feeble strength. He was seized with a fit of coughing, and went off, poor fellow, like a lamb, after giving me this sealed packet of MS, which he solemnly enjoined me to read." As he finished he showed the packet to Nurse Everest, and continued: "It promises to be a long story, so I am going to sit down and devour it slowly over a pipe."

"Very well, Sir Ashleigh; then I will leave you alone until you want me; I shall be close at hand." As she said this she closed the door of the patient's room, leaving him comfortably seated by the fire with his back to me window. He first cut up some plug tobacco, filled his pipe, and, after lighting it successfully, broke the seal of the packet, and began to read it slowly. Luckily it was written in a clear, distinct hand. Two or three letters and other papers fell at his feet; they were in different hand-writings. He examined each in turn, and after a little hesitation, decided to begin with the MS.

"I, Jabez Waldegrave, being of sound mind, do hereby certify that the following record is strictly true:

"I was born in the year 1820, in the village of ———, and baptized in the Church of St John's, in the parish of ———. My father, who was a clergyman before me, early destined me for the Church. I was educated at Eton, took my degree at Oxford, and finally settled down in my native village, where I eventually succeeded my father in the ministry, married at the age of thirty-five a lady of good family, and brought up nine children, all of whom are now married and scattered over me face of the earth.

"My own life from the time I entered the ministry—in fact, I may say from so far back as I could remember—had been singularly uneventful, passed chiefly in the village, which is one of the slowest and most backward places in the kingdom. People did not travel then as they do now; and my means being slender, and soon having an increasing family to support, I had to be strictly economical in expenditure. My mother died when I was only sixteen, leaving behind her myself and two sisters, Lucy and Martha, both older than I, and who married soon after our loss.

"My maternal uncle, Aubrey de Vere, who, as I have heard my father say, was colonel of the ——— Lancers, and present at the storming of Seringapatam, formerly the capital of the Mysore State, and the stronghold of Tippoo Sahib, who fell fighting gallantly for his liberty in the year 1799. Now, it happened that in the midst of the misery and massacre that followed the attack, for the stronghold had been fired, and few escaped with their lives, that a woman, with her head closely wrapped in a shawl, presented herself at the opening of the tent of Colonel Aubrey de Vere, and piteously begged for her life and protection from the lawlessness of the soldiers. Colonel de Vere, who was a kindhearted man, told her to rise and uncover her face.

"And when he saw that she was young and extremely beautiful, he began to take an interest in her, and questioned her closely. She told him the following pathetic story:

"She was one of the ladies of the Zenana of the late Tippoo Sahib. When the place was stormed, the women were driven forth, and subjected to the insults of the soldiers. Dreading to fall into their hands, she, with great address, eluded them, and making her way to de Vere's tent, appealed to him as a gentleman and a man of honour for protection. She added that she had been forced to become one of the wives of Tippoo Sahib; and had, indeed, been brought to him by pirates, who had captured her in a distant country, and sold her to him. Her name was Zoraida, and she was known and spoken of as the Pearl of the East. The pirates had torn her from the arms of the man she loved, and had slaughtered him before her eyes. She did not love her purchaser, although he lavished the richest jewels and other presents on her, and would have made her Queen of the Zenana, had she returned his passion. The other ladies of the harem envied and hated her, and treated her spitefully. She loathed her position, and had often longed to escape, when, lo, it had pleased Allah that the English should storm the fortress and set her free. She said, and her beautiful black eyes filled with tears as she spoke, that she would worship the brave man who would free her from the degradation of her late position. Yes, she would follow him through the world all her life, and gladly be his slave. So eloquent were her words, and so overwhelming the fascination of her delicate and exquisitely graceful form and features, that the chivalrous colonel promised her his protection; and, indeed, subsequently married her.

"I have enclosed with this story a letter from de Vere to my mother, announcing his engagement to the most beautiful woman the world had ever known, and also of his intention of bringing her to England, and introducing her to his family.

"The letter, you will notice, is dated 1799."

Here Carruthers discontinued his reading to find the letter referred to, which he perused. It contained little more than what he had already read. He laid it aside and resumed the perusal of the MS.

"This, I say, was his full intention at the time he wrote; but, alas, he never returned to England! He appears to have died suddenly in a strange, mysterious way. One report was to the effect that he had been bitten, while in a deep sleep, by a vampire bat, and bled to death before any help could be summoned; but he had made a will a little before his demise, a copy of which is with this paper."

•••

CHAPTER XII

A REMARKABLE STORY

C arruthers broke off here to look for the will, which he carefully read. It was not a long one, but accurately drawn, dated
only a few days before de Vere's death, and bequeathed all he
possessed to his beloved wife.

Carruthers continued his reading of the MS.

"A year later Mrs. de Vere, the widow, arrived in England, and introduced herself to her husband's family. She told them a very remarkable
story.

"The vessel in which. she had set sail for England had been wrecked,
and all hands on board had perished except herself. The loss of the vessel had been reported, yet no mention had been made of her having
been saved. On the contrary, all on board had been stated to have been
drowned. There were some people who doubted the truth of the tale so
plausibly related by the handsome widow, and even warned Colonel de
Vere's family against her, whom they described as an adventuress.

"Mrs. de Vere was, however, equal to the occasion, and, without
hesitation, produced undeniable proof of her identity in the shape of
her late husband's will, the certificate of her marriage, his medals, and
certain family relics, which were at once recognised by his mother. All
the doubts even of the most sceptical being thus swept away, she was
received into the bosom of her husband's family with every show of
affection, and her romantic story of her wonderful escape from the
wreck was implicitly believed.

"Mrs. de Vere dressed in the deepest mourning and appeared inconsolable for the loss of her husband. This trait alone endeared her to the family, and all its members condoled with her, and spoke of her in the most affectionate terms. There was one member of the family, however, who stood out against the fascinations of the new-comer; and that was a maiden aunt of mine, Janet, my mother's only unmarried sister, whose religious orthodoxy and general rigid sense of propriety caused her to hold all expressions of goodwill or affection in check until persons had first proved themselves worthy of her favour. Aunt Janet first hinted that Mrs. de Vere, being an alien, had in all probability never been baptised. Her extraordinary physical beauty and distinction were rather against her, as likely to lead to disquieting results in the peaceful minds of the inhabitants of the village. Her fascination of manner and originality in conversation might all be used for evil purposes. It is hardly necessary to state that Aunt Janet was neither beautiful nor fascinating. On one occasion Aunt Janet, who was characteristically bent upon solving the mystery of Mrs. de Vere's proper admission into the church's fold, put the question with the most brutal frankness. With a flash in her black eyes, but without the slightest hesitation, Mrs. Aubrey de Vere drew from her pocket a copy of her baptismal certificate, in which her original name: of Zoraida had been changed to Amanda Christina Maria."

This paper Carruthers also verified with the other documents.

"Aunt Janet was a little checked by the promptitude with which her attacks had been answered; but, as if she still doubted the genuineness of Mrs. de Vere's orthodoxy, she began questioning her on the leading articles of Christianity.

"'Oh, yes, I know perfectly well what you Christians believe in,' replied Mrs. Aubrey de Vere, flippantly, 'there is the Lord's Prayer, and the Creed, and the Commandments; yes, and the Eucharist. If you don't believe me I can repeat them all correctly. Why, I've committed all the Thirty-nine Articles to memory. I'll repeat them all till you are tired.' And the widow began rattling them off one after another just like a Sunday school child repeating a lesson; and, as Aunt Janet, with pious indignation, observed afterwards, without a particle of reverence. In spite of this, however, it was necessary to admit that she was well-informed on all she professed to believe; she was perfect in the letter, but the spirit was a minus quantity.

"Mrs. de Vere not only proved her knowledge of dogma, but she displayed an amount of acute intelligence that startled everyone. Her knowledge of history and geography was prodigious. She was acquainted with the early history of every nation in Europe, and, in addition, her mastery of Eastern lore and language passed belief. Her English was admirable, and she could speak most of the European tongues. Her wit and power of repartee were dreaded by opponents; and, as to argument, Aunt Janet soon found herself mastered and compelled to submit.

"She was, however, too combative to give up the contest; and thought it unnatural that one so young—she only looked eighteen, though she confessed to be twenty—could have acquired so much extraordinary knowledge, whatever pains had been bestowed upon her education.

"'Might not all this learning have come to her from the Evil One?' thought the old lady, who had a potent belief in the supreme power of the lower regions. She resolved to put this to the test, and would entice Mrs. de Vere to church and study her demeanour there; and Aunt Janet's suspicion gained strength when she found that by one excuse or another, Mrs. de Vere evaded her carefully prepared traps. She also showed great skill in eluding all attempts to involve her in theological argument. Mrs. de Vere referred to the Christian religion in a way which shocked the acute orthodoxy of Aunt Janet as one of the creeds—a very good one in its way no doubt—but it must be admitted that there were others quite as good and a great deal older. It hadn't even the merit of originality, and had very manifestly been compiled from more ancient beliefs; in fact, it might fairly be characterised as an eclectic faith.

"It would be impossible to do justice to the pious fury aroused in Aunt Janet by such terrible, and, to her, blasphemous opinions.

"She roundly declared this young widow, who was dangerously fascinating and strangely beautiful, to be no Christian at all except in name; but, on the contrary, as much a benighted heathen in heart as if she had never been baptised; and then, thinking her outside the pale of the Church, she turned her back upon her.

"In addition to Mrs. de Vere's indifference to religion, there was another trait in her character which caused surprise to the members of her late husband's family, and that was her marked love of solitude. She expressed a desire to occupy a small house which stood in a very lonely situation, and to be attended by only one servant. This idea was violently combated by all the family as one quite out of character for a lady of her position, age, and attractions. They all pointed out to her, with much unction, the danger of such a position, its solitude, and its unsociability.

"She replied coolly that she loved solitude, that she had been accustomed to it from her youth, that she could pursue her studies without interruption, and finally that the resources she had in herself would prevent the possibility of her being unhappy. This extraordinary statement, which was made with an air of quiet conviction, made her new family realise once and for all that Mrs. Aubrey de Vere was a lady of a very abnormal kind, who was always successful in doing as she pleased.

"After a formal protest and reprimand, which the lady treated with an air of gentle ridicule, they admitted her perfect right to have her own way, rightly feeling that it would be useless to oppose her further. In addition to this, the members of the family felt at the bottom of their hearts a sense of unspoken relief at the idea of this singular woman's departure. Her character, her principles, if she had any, her opinions, her ways and manners; in short, her utter disregard of all the plausible conventionalities of country life, were a constant offence to the members of the family into which she had entered in so extraordinary a manner.

"All discussion ended in Mrs. Aubrey de Vere renting a small house in a most solitary part of the county, so far away as to make it a little difficult for those she had left to visit her often. She had one maid of all work to wait upon her. Though in comfortable circumstances, she incurred no unnecessary expense, and the local tradespeople soon summed her up as excessively 'near.' Her bills were ridiculously small; and the food sent in appeared hardly enough for one person; indeed, the well-fed butcher, baker, and grocer expressed their wonder that two people could keep bodies and souls together on the nutriment supplied. One other remarkable fact about Mrs. de Vere was that no one ever saw her eat.

"The members of the de Vere family had at first been seriously alarmed at her lack of appetite, for she merely played with her food, and was never seen to swallow anything. She would frequently excuse herself from coming to lunch or dinner, by pleading headache or some other ailment. And when present on those occasions would resist all the pressing of the family, who were, including the orthodox Aunt Janet, possessed of fine, robust, country appetites."

•••

CHAPTER XIII

MRS. AUBREY DE VERE
AT HOME

◯

As week after week passed and my uncle's widow persisted in her abstinence from food, the family became alarmed, thinking that no one could be in good health who refused all proper nutriment. It ended in their resolving on consulting a doctor; but feeling certain that she would refuse his advice or assistance, they took it upon themselves to call in a medical man and introduce him to Mrs. Aubrey de Vere as a friend of the family. But she at once saw through the deception and coloured deeply with indignation; stoutly affirming that she had never consulted a doctor in the whole course of her life; that she understood perfectly her own constitution; and that she would thank them in future to leave the care of her health to her own knowledge and experience.

"This was the first ebullition of temper she had ever shown them; but it had the effect of convincing the family that she had a strong will of her own and intended to exercise it.

"But when the little outburst had passed off, she consented to be examined by the eminent London practitioner who had been sent for; and, he, after a careful examination, declared her heart, lungs, and constitution generally to be in perfect condition.

"The only one who protested against the doctor's opinion was Aunt Janet, who prided herself on what she imagined she knew of medicine, and had, indeed, dosed the whole family with her old-fashioned nostrums for years.

"'You may say what you please, doctor,' she protested, 'but I maintain that no person with breath so offensive as Mrs. de Vere's can by any possibility be in a good state of health.'

"Then, turning to the widow herself, she added: 'Whether you may like to hear it or not, my dear, it is my duty to inform you that your breath smells—well, like nothing so much as a graveyard.'

"Mrs. de Vere had been angry before at the introduction of the doctor; but her fury at this statement of her old opponent amounted to the frenzy of a maniac.

"How dared she insult her by such a gross calumny! It was false. She thanked heaven that her breath was as sweet as a rose and always had been; it must be her own (Aunt Janet's) breath that was in her own nostrils and caused her to believe it was someone else's.

"The doctor merely smiled, for he had detected the unpleasant peculiarity, and suggested a mild tonic to promote appetite, and took his departure.

"After this experience of Mrs. de Vere's temper and character it is not surprising that the family with which she had been staying felt a very mitigated sorrow at her departure.

"The widow settled in her little house with one maidservant only to attend her. She was a raw country girl still in her teens, a poor waif and orphan, who had neither relation nor friend, and had always appeared to be in everyone's way, about whose education and moral training no one had troubled. Although rough and plain in appearance, Nature had bestowed on her a good, grateful heart and a splendid constitution.

"What could have induced the graceful, aristocratic-looking Mrs. Aubrey de Vere to select out of the many persons who applied for the situation, this rough, uncouth daughter of the soil, this unmistakable hewer of wood? That was only known to herself. As to Madge, she could hardly believe in the good luck that had befallen her, and when this, to her, grand and beautiful lady first spoke kindly, and then engaged her on the spot, it appeared to Madge that an angel had descended from Heaven to help and sympathise with her forlorn condition. She had never listened to kind words, and been the recipient of kind looks; and, now, this sweet and gracious lady, whose beauty had surpassed anything Madge could have imagined, bestowed both on her. The consequence of this was that Madge, who had always hungered and thirsted for kindness and sympathy, adored her mistress with the unreasoning devotion of an animal; and was never tired of hoarsely singing her praises to any of her acquaintances who would listen.

"Some weeks passed away, during which time Madge served her new mistress like a most devoted slave. Her duties were, of course, entirely domestic, and of the roughest kind; but what did she care? To be for once in her life well clothed, and paid; and, above everything else, to be allowed, at times, to be in this grand lady's company, to listen to her voice, and to gaze at her brilliant black eyes and beautiful features, was to poor Madge the only real delight she had ever enjoyed. She had never known before what it was to be treated like a human being endowed with the ordinary qualities of humanity. Everything appeared new to her; she felt as if she were raised out of a deep, dark pit into radiant sunshine, when her beautiful mistress's lustrous eyes beamed softly on her. . . .

"'Why, Madge,' said the village butcher, on one occasion, when the girl was in his shop, 'your mistress isn't much of a customer to me. Why she hardly orders enough meat for one person with a small appetite.'

"''Cause there is only one person,' replied Madge. 'I eats it all. My mistress never touches it! She be too much of an angel!'

"'Never touches meat!' exclaimed the scandalised and outraged butcher. 'What! and a rich lady, too! Well, I'm blowed if she ain't a mean cat!'

"'Oh, no, she ain't a bit mean, she ain't,' protested the faithful Madge. 'Why, she's the kindest, dearest, and most generous soul as ever lived in the world, that's what my mistress be. If it wasn't for her—'

"'Then,' interrupted the man of meat, 'why don't she show it by livin' decent like a lady. I means feeding proper like all honest folk.'

"'She doesn't take to it, dear soul,' replied the girl. 'I cooks it every day and serves it; but I never once seed her touch none of it; no, never once. She just pushes it away from her, and says to me, she does, "There, Madge, you may eat that"; and so I does, I just eats it all.'

"'What do she eat, then?' inquired the wondering butcher.

"'Nothin' as I knows on. I never asks no questions; but she's a dear lady, and I know she be fond of me,' replied Madge.

"'Well, that's as rum a go as ever I know'd,' remarked the butcher, and the conversation ended.

"Madge in her new house was perfectly happy, and soon from looking wretched and half-starved became fat and sleek and almost good-looking. This was remarked by her former acquaintances in the village, when she made her appearance there; and she was hated and envied in consequence.

"But people saw very little of either mistress or maid; although after a time reports were spread that Madge, who had been looking so well and fat, had relapsed to a condition worse than she was in before entering Mrs. de Vere's service. When questioned by the curious, however, she would answer no questions about either herself or her mistress. She had learned to be reticent. It was observed by those who occasionally met her that she lost flesh day by day, and grew visibly worse. Soon after that she was reported to be dead. Some said it was a decline; others that the change of life had not agreed with her.

"But naturally very little interest was taken in the death of a poor, ignorant girl like Madge. None cared for her when living, and why should anyone trouble about her death? So the girl was buried in a nameless grave, one of many similar ones, in an old-fashioned cemetery, and forgotten. Mrs. Aubrey de Vere engaged an elderly woman as caretaker of the cottage, and announced her intention of travelling abroad."

• • •

CHAPTER XIV

IN THE FULL LIGHT
OF THE MOON

◇

When Carruthers had read the MS to this point, he stopped, knocked the ashes from his pipe, and began thinking aloud: "Begad! it's the same woman; I'll swear to that! There could not be two such monsters on the face of the earth at the same time! Why everything goes to prove it: her fascinating, almost unique beauty, her abominable breath, her intellect and independence of character, her utter heartlessness—yes, yes, all proves, without leaving room for the shadow of a doubt, that it is the same creature. . . ." Carruthers carefully filled his pipe, thinking furiously all the time. "And it is wonderful to be compelled to believe this woman was twenty years of age at the storming of Seringapatam in 1799; and now we are in the year 1901, which proves her to be over one hundred and twenty years old at this moment! Good Heavens! what a thing to take into one's brain and admit to be true! . . . In spite of the overwhelming fact of her age, she only looks eighteen! . . . Such things surpass the scope of human comprehension. . . . Yet, I am not dreaming. No, my pipe is in my mouth and I am sitting here in the full possession of my reasoning powers."

When Carruthers had arrived at this consoling reflection, a knock was heard at the door, and, on Carruthers saying "Come in!" Nurse Everest entered with a daintily prepared luncheon. When this had been despatched, with due enjoyment, Carruthers said:

"I have just been reading this MS, and it contains matter that will interest you. I haven't finished it—for it is a long story; but when I have done so you shall read it."

"I should like to do so, Sir Ashleigh, very much." Then, noticing the animated expression of his countenance, she inquired, in an agitated tone of voice: "Does it throw any light on that——?"

"What, upon that female vampire?" he interrupted. "Yes, that is exactly what it does do; but I can't tell you all about it in a few words."

Carruthers asked her to sit down. And he began the conversation by inquiring whether the hideous dream still continued to return.

"It was only last night," she replied, "that I had another very remarkable one."

"Tell me all about it, nurse," interrupted Carruthers, excitedly.

"I thought that I was in a cemetery and it was night, for the full moon was shining on the tombstones and casting weird shadows from the yews and cypresses that were thickly planted near the graves. At first I seemed to be alone. Then I heard in the deep silence the church clock boom out the hour of midnight. As the last stroke vibrated in the air a female figure, veiled, and dressed in black from head to foot, made her way towards me from between the graves. She did not see me; and evidently thinking herself alone, threw her veil aside, and by her gestures I saw that she was plunged in the depths of despair. The moon at that moment shone full upon her deathly pale face and large, lustrous eyes; and, with a shudder, I recognised the accursed features of that fiendish woman who makes my very soul thrill with horror. There she stood only separated from me by a few feet, in all her unholy beauty. Oh, how I loathe her! Why, I asked myself, was it ever permitted that one with a heart so black should masquerade in so angelic a form?

"At length, after many gestures of despair, she spoke, still unaware of my presence. I listened, with every nerve at the highest degree of tension, hidden under the dark shadow of a cypress, and distinctly heard the following words:

"'What! Have I not repeatedly died, and been buried, and yet triumphed over death and the grave? Have I not risen again, not indeed to the life eternal, like those who possess a soul; but at least to the life of the body with its sensuous delights? Have I not left sheath after sheath of my material self to moulder in the grave, while my astral body has been permitted by the infernal powers to walk the earth, and to cover itself with a new visible and palpable sheath at will?... And I have succeeded in maintaining this form by drawing from living mortals the very essence of their lives! Have I not been aided and sustained in this by the magic properties of the ring I stole from the mummy of the great Egyptian adept? But now, woe is me! That is gone, and I must die for ever!

"'Must I no more enjoy the light and the warmth of the glorious sun; must I lose all the keen and vivid pleasures of life? What! Become extinct and have no more sensation than those dull stones! Oh! to possess a soul once more! Alas, alas, it is too late!... I prayed for a body; one that would not die! My prayer was answered. The possession of the ring secured me that.... Now that is gone; and I shall no longer be able to take upon me a human form of seductive grace and beauty; but be condemned to wander and crawl about at night in the loathsome form of a bat or creeping reptile!'

"Here the abominable creature threw up her arms in mad desperation; then fell prostrate on a low grave and writhed like a wounded serpent in her anguish. After a time she rose to her feet and resumed her lamentations:

"'Lost, lost for ever!... This present form cannot endure! As I speak it withers!'

"Then as I gazed on her writhing face and form in the full light of the moon I distinctly saw a horrible, incredible change in both; the fair, pale skin grew yellow and wrinkled; the lustrous large black eyes sank deeply in her head, the luxuriant black hair grew thin and white, her cheeks became hollow, her upright graceful figure appeared bowed and bony, and, in short there stood before me, instead of an exquisitely beautiful woman, a decrepit, sordid-looking hag, who gasped and mumbled out as if with her last breath: 'Oh, the ring, the ring, or I die for ever!'

"Then she dwindled and dwindled away, till she became nothing but a mere skeleton; and the bones became dust; and then, a terrible whirlwind stormed through the place of death which swept away her last remains!"

Carruthers was unable to speak for some time after the nurse had finished her terrible dream. All he could say was, "That, indeed, was an awful vision, nurse!"

• • •

CHAPTER XV
THE TEMPTRESS

◯

Captain Carruthers resumed his reading of the story after Nurse Everest had retired. "Let me see," he said, "where did I leave off? Ah! I remember, the creature avowed her intention of going abroad."

"I must now pass over a period of forty years. I had by this time reached the age of twenty, and had commenced my career. My mother had been dead for years, and my sisters were married. I alone was left at home to cheer my father's declining days. We saw no company to speak of, and as our few friends and connections lived some distance away, we saw little of them, which did not trouble us. My father and myself were consequently much alone together; and we often beguiled the time by a game of chess or backgammon. He, like most men of his age, was fond of recalling the events of the past, and would often tell me good stories of his College life, his courtship of my mother, her family, and especially of her brother, Colonel Aubrey de Vere, and his strangely beautiful wife. There was a mystery about Mrs. de Vere that greatly excited my youthful imagination. Her sudden appearance on the scene after the storming of Seringapatam, her mysterious disappearance soon after, for since she left England, her husband's family had beard nothing whatever about her, her bankers alone hearing from her purely on business matters; all this increased my interest in her strange personality.

"There were, in addition, curious and dark reports afloat amongst the villagers with regard to this lady, both before and after she was supposed to have left England. I am not inclined, as a rule, to listen to local gossip or to encourage the villagers in their ignorance and superstition. I now merely repeat certain things that were said without note or comment. What follows proves that they were not without some foundation in fact.

"One story was to the effect that she had been seen wandering about at night in solitary places long after she was supposed to have left the country; and also that in those cottages which happened to be near the places where people had seen her, some members of the families living in them, always the youngest, were noticed to die in a mysterious manner; in fact, it became a common saying in the country-side, when a young person or child died suddenly, that they had had a visit from the 'Black Lady' or the 'Lady in Black.' Desolation and death were said to follow in her track; she was also credited with the power of making herself visible or invisible at will; and, in addition, of appearing in two places at one and the same time. Many of the villagers said she was a witch, and ought to be burnt alive. All those mysterious and, apparently, incredible things were said to have occurred before I was born, and nothing had been heard of Mrs. de Vere for forty years; so that only the oldest people in the village believed in the strange stories of the 'Woman in Black.' These old people were considered by the rising generation to be in their dotage; and those who pretended to possess the advantages of modern education scoffed at them. My father, however, was one of the old school, and although he would not exactly commit himself by admitting that he believed in all the old rustic gossip, he nevertheless, by a mysterious hint or shake of the head, induced me to think that much, if not all, of these rumours had, in his opinion, facts to support them. He was fond of quoting the well-worn lines: 'There are more things in heaven and earth, Horatio, than are dreamed of in your philosophy.'

"On one occasion he said to me, 'My son, if ever you should meet that woman, shun her as you would a pest. Let her not take thee, in the words of Solomon, with her eyelids.'

"'Why, father,' I said laughingly, 'if she is alive today she is sixty years of age.'

"'Nevertheless, beware! She may be nearer to you than you imagine,' he added in solemn tones; and I had soon cause to remember the warning, but at the time, in the arrogance of my youth, ignorance, and health, I recollect thinking that my father must be a little weak and wandering in his mind. Alas, would that I had taken his advice! ·

"At about this time there was a county ball near, and all the best families in the neighbourhood were gathered together there. Many of the men were in hunting dress. The ladies in those days wore short-waisted dresses, and topknots. Being young, although in orders, I was present. As I walked through the crowded room I found everyone's attention directed to a young lady of marvellous distinction, grace, and beauty, who did not appear to be more than twenty years of age. She was seated in a graceful attitude upon a sofa surrounded by a group of young men in pink, who were standing or lolling about in various postures, intent on every word she uttered, and apparently treating her with the worship due to a divinity, while the other neglected women stood aloof and gazed at the evident belle of the ball with envy and dislike.

"As I approached the lady and her worshippers, and gazed upon her exquisite features and beautiful form, I appeared to be bewitched by the same fascination that had subdued the other men; for love is a plant of quick growth when one is twenty, and I felt compelled to linger there. Yes, I thought it was love, like many a young man full of simplicity and altogether empty of worldly experience.

"Bah! When I look back now, I am fully aware that it was no more love than the attraction exercised on the bird by the snake, or the load-stone on steel. But, at the same time, it was all-powerful. From the first moment that her mysteriously beautiful black eyes fell and rested upon me, I was her abject slave. All the other men who crowded around her seemed equally smitten. A friend of mine, who had joined the group, observing my approach, addressed me by name, whereupon the lady looked up, and, scorning conventionality, extended her hand to me, and partly rising, said:

"'I should have known you anywhere, Mr. Waldegrave, from your likeness to your father. I knew him well when he was a young man of your age; of course, before you were born.'

"I blushed and felt foolish, and doubtless looked so.

"'Come, come, Mrs. de Vere,' said laughingly, several young men in a breath. 'That won't do, you know; that's really too steep; of course, you're making fun of us. Why, how old do you want to make yourself?'

"'Perhaps I am older than you have any idea,' she replied, with a dazzlingly beautiful smile. 'I first came over from India in the year 1800, a year after the storming of Seringapatam. This gentleman was not born until twenty years later, so that he is now twenty. I myself was also twenty, or supposed to be,' she added, *sotto voce*.

"'Now make up that little sum in simple addition, and tell me what it comes to.'

"'Mrs. de Vere, you cannot really mean us to believe that you, who are now in the very flower of youth and loveliness, are sixty years of age!' protested one of her admirers. 'That would, indeed, be too great a tax upon even our faith.'

"'Ask this gentleman's father to tell you the truth, if you doubt my word,' she added in a very quiet tone of voice.

"'Then all I can say is that your make up is more than wonderful,' remarked another, whose face expressed his utter disbelief in her statement.

"At this moment the warning of my father arose in my mind. He had solemnly cautioned me against the extraordinary fascinations of this very woman; and I had mentally ridiculed the preposterous idea of falling in love with a woman of sixty! Yet, in spite of that, I felt I was in the snare. My heart had been hers from the first moment I met her eyes. Whenever she rose or wherever she went, the men followed her, as if irresistibly drawn by a powerful magnet; but, strange to say, she seemed to favour me above all me rest. This was embarrassing, as

I was painfully conscious of my want of physical attractions, of conversational resources; and was timid and awkward in my bearing and movements as a necessary consequence. How was it possible she could prefer me, a lanky student, with pale face and sloping shoulders, to those handsome, well set up, and fresh-complexioned men, in their exquisitely fitting clothes, which set off their manly proportions to the best advantage? In spite of that, this beautiful idolised creature lavished her favours and sweetest smiles on me. Was that not enough to turn a stronger head than mine; and make a man forget all the warnings given by all the fathers who had ever lived?

"The other aspirants for the lady's smiles turned their glances on me in anger and bewilderment; then looked at each other in the hope of finding some explanation of the enigma. I cared nothing for their indignation; but inspired with temporary boldness by her kindness to me, I engaged her hand for the next waltz. Oh, how divinely she danced! It was, indeed, the very poetry of motion. Before long, however, my poor head swam and my legs bent till I was compelled to pray for a respite. She, who had danced as if she would never be tired, and indeed appeared to half glide and half fly round the room, laughingly acceded to my request and we strolled into a conservatory together. Here, hidden by exotic large-leaved plants, we chatted together in the most delightful and familiar way; at least, it appeared so to me, although nearly all the charming talk was on her side, for I was ever a poor stick at conversation, especially with the opposite sex; but in spite of that I felt intensely happy with her.

"We were at length discovered by a dashing young squire who had engaged her for a dance; and walked off with her on bis arm. She, however, gave me one fond, lingering glance as she left the conservatory, which made my foolish heart palpitate, as it appeared to me to indicate that she preferred my company to any other. When alone, I reflected on what had passed, having no desire to dance with any other lady; and, indeed, could think only of the exquisite woman who had bewitched me. Had she been so gracious to me merely because she had known my father? Was there nothing more than that in her favour? Even if she loved me as I loved her, and she appeared to do so, how could I, a poor curate, with my pitiful income, ask her to marry me? The idea was absurd. Of course, I had forgotten that she was my late uncle's widow! and, by her own admission, sixty years of age. My father's warning words directing me to shun her as a pest, if we even met, were also forgotten.

"My wild, unreasonable passion swept all this away. I thought only of her beauty, her wit, her grace, her unspeakable fascinations; and was, above all, and everything, intoxicated by the insane belief that she loved me! That was all I now lived and longed for. After all these ideas and feelings had passed through my mind and heart, I went in search of her, and, on finding her, we went into supper together. She would, however, partake of nothing. I, on the other hand, although I ate very little, drank too much in my feverish excitement. We soon strolled back into the conservatory; and by that time we had grown as intimate as the closest friends. In the midst of our animated conversation she rose suddenly, and opening her white, smooth, beautifully shaped arms, she impetuously twined them round my neck, exclaiming as she did so: 'Oh, my dear boy, how I love you!' kissing me on the lips with long, passionate kisses at the same time. 'Don't think that any of those silly men are anything to me. I love you—you only! Oh, take me, I am yours.'

"I knew no more—my head reeled. I staggered after her as she suddenly left me; but failed to overtake her; she appeared to disappear in the crowd. I felt all my strength and self-consciousness abandon me, and must have finally fallen insensible on a couch."

• • •

CHAPTER XVI

FATHER AND SON

I cannot remember how I reached home, but I rose the next morning feeling very weak: my head ached, my eyes were bloodshot, and when I came down for breakfast, I thought my father looked at me very suspiciously.

"'Well,' he said, after a pause, 'did you enjoy yourself last night? The supper of course was good?'

"I nodded in acquiescence.

"'You danced, I suppose?' he added.

"I admitted that I had done so.

"'Tell me,' he said, dropping his light tone, and lowering his voice: 'Was she there?'

"'She? Who?' I returned, trying to look innocent and indifferent, but blushing to the roots of my hair.

"My father, who was a great stickler for absolute truth, and could not brook the slightest deviation from it, replied severely, 'You need not try to prevaricate with me, sir. You know perfectly well whom I mean; the woman I warned you against.'

"'Sir,' I replied, 'I will not attempt to deny it; she was there.'

"'Then all is explained? I need not ask more,' he said. 'My poor boy! I pity you!'

"I suppose I looked astonished at these words, for, as if in answer to an inquiring look, he continued:

"'Now, would you be very much surprised if I, though absent from the ball, should be able to tell you exactly what happened there?'

"'I should, indeed,' I answered.

"'Well, then, this is what occurred: When you entered the ball-room, you found her seated in the centre of a crowd of admirers of your own sex, looking young, beautiful, and fresh as a girl of eighteen. She was graceful and vivacious, and her troop of worshippers hung greedily upon her every word and look. Was that not so?'

"'It is true, sir,' I answered.

"'Hearing your name, she addressed you, at once, without waiting for an introduction; and, immediately lavished upon you her choicest smiles and sweetest words for the rest of the evening. You danced with her, and she tired you so nearly to death that you were obliged to ask for quarter. Her beauty fascinated you, her conversation charmed you, and after the pause in the dancing, you led her to a conservatory.'

"'Sir, you amaze me!' I exclaimed in astonishment. 'How did you——?'

"'One moment,' he continued, interrupting me. 'You then took her into supper and offered her refreshment; but she partook of nothing. You, on the contrary, drank to excess.'

"Here I blushed and hung my head.

"'After which,' he proceeded, 'you returned to the conservatory, and—and—strange as it may seem—in your half-intoxicated condition she actually had the effrontery to open her arms, clasp you round the neck, and kiss you passionately on the lips, at the same time avowing her love for you, and adding that the attentions of all the other men were nothing to her, as she loved you alone. Is not that all true?'

"'Father! father!' I exclaimed, losing all control over myself and bursting into tears. 'Yes: all you say is as true as if you had been there and seen and heard everything! But how did you know—how could you know?'

"'My boy,' he answered, 'age brings experience. I know it because I know her. She behaved in the same way to me when I was your age; before you were born; and, indeed, before I had set my eyes on your mother. It is now forty years ago. She looks now just as young as she did then; and doubtless she will look the same till the end of her time on earth. Yes, my son, your old father was one of her dupes, and I am not surprised that you should likewise succumb.'

"Had a thunderbolt fallen at my feet I should not have been more astonished than I was at hearing this tale from my father's own lips. Who and what was this mysterious woman who appeared to possess the power of living on in perpetual youth and beauty in utter defiance of nature and time? Was she woman or was she fiend? What could be her motive in ensnaring both father and son? My curiosity was aroused and I plied my father with questions. It was humiliating to think that we had both been bewitched by the same creature. I cannot well describe my feelings for her after my father's story. I loathed her for her deceit and wickedness; but I could not help admiring her exquisite beauty of form and face; neither could I tear out the poisoned barb of passion that rankled in my heart. The consequence of this mixed, almost insane, feeling was that I fell into a kind of decline; and for a long time my life was in great danger.

"My father, who was a deeply religious man, devoted himself to me during my illness. He prayed over me day and night; and I attribute my recovery more to his unceasing prayers that I might be spared to him than to the medical aid given to me. I saw no more of the mysterious woman; neither did my father. Many inquiries were made about her, for the sensation she had made at the ball was not easily forgotten; but nothing could be heard of her. There was one strange circumstance, however. Renewed reports were circulated of the sudden deaths of children and young people similar to those of forty years ago. In concluding this extraordinary narrative, I will mention a remarkable experience of my own. One night, I being then convalescent, when just about to retire to rest, my attention was attracted by something beating against my window panes; it sounded like some nightbird trying to enter. Curiosity induced me to open the window, when to my surprise, an enormous bat of the vampire species, such as are unknown in these parts, flew in. It flew straight at my throat, where it fastened its teeth; and, at the same time, I felt a kind of numbness stealing over me, which deprived me of all my will power; and, indeed, began to lull me to sleep. Rousing myself, however, by an almost superhuman effort, I drove it away, and seizing a poker, dealt it a heavy blow, at which, with a shriek, it dashed through the still open window, and vanished into the darkness of night. When I had closed the window, I noticed a stain of blood on my night-shirt; and did my best to staunch the wound from which it flowed. After that I informed my father of what had happened, and he told me that forty years ago he had had a similar experience, with very serious results to his health. The vampire, in his case, had concealed itself in the curtains of his bedroom, and attacked him in the night during sleep, so that he narrowly escaped bleeding to death. This event recalled to our memory the reports circulated in my uncle's (Col. Aubrey de Vere's) regiment, that he had met his death, shortly after his marriage, through being bitten by a vampire bat. It is hardly necessary to add that both my father and myself slept with our windows closed after what I have related occurred."

Here ended the Rev. Jabez Waldegrave's extraordinary story.

But as Carruthers was folding the sheets, he noticed some lines written in pencil on the outside of the last one. They were dated the day before the vicar's death, and ran as follows:

"To my young friend, Ashleigh Carruthers, I dedicate this narrative in token of the love I bear to the memory of his father, Sir Hugh, my friend and benefactor, in the hope that a perusal of the same may avert those machinations of the Evil One to which myself and my family have fallen victims.

(Signed) Jabez Waldegrave,
Vicar of St. Cuthbert's in the Parish
July 1899."

* * * * *

When Carruthers had finished reading the last kind message sent by the man now dead, he began to pace the room, thinking deeply: "How all the evidence seems to fit together in order to point out and condemn the creature! How full of suggestion are the dreams of Nurse Everest! Then, alas, the warning of Phyllis; I am certain it was her voice I heard on that terrible night; it still rings in my ears. . . . Poor little Phyllis! Yes, she too was a victim! . . . No wonder her father set her death down to witchcraft. He was right. If ever there was a witch that woman is one! 'Thou shalt not suffer a witch to live,' the Bible says. A very sensible injunction, too. For if a witch, such a one as this creature, means a body that has lost its soul and can only continue its accursed existence by drawing, vampire-like, the life essence of innocent mortals, and thus driving them into the grave, who would dare to deny that such a monster ought to be stamped out of existence? And, what is more, if I can assist in carrying out this laudable object, I will gladly devote all my best energies to the task!"

At this moment a gentle knock was heard at the door. "Come in," said Carruthers; and Nurse Everest entered.

"Did you call, Sir Ashleigh?" she inquired. "I thought I heard you."

"No, nurse, I did not call you; but now you are here, you may as well sit down and read this," handing her the MS, "and tell me what is your opinion of it. A little outing will do me good, I think, so I shall take a short stroll with the help of my stick; and you can read quietly in the meanwhile."

Carruthers, without another word, left the room.

• • •

CHAPTER XVII
INSPECTOR JONES

D
r. Leach paid Carruthers his farewell visit the next morning, and told him that he was quite convalescent; and, in fact, well enough to return home.

The further services of Nurse Everest were consequently not required, and it became necessary to bid her farewell. This Carruthers did, after thanking her very warmly for her great skill, care, tact, and kindness, and shaking her hand warmly; in fact, he held her little hand in his longer than was necessary, and there was even a little moisture in his eyes as she turned to leave the room. Just as she opened the door he said:

"I don't mean to lose sight of you, nurse, and if ever I require your services again—why, I have your London address, and I will send for you. I will also recommend you to my friends."

"Thank you, Sir Ashleigh," said the nurse, while the colour rose in her cheeks as she saw the light in Carruthers' eyes and felt the late warm pressure of his hand tingle through her frame. Her own eyes shone with that liquid light which is the most exquisite charm of a pretty woman's face. "Thank you ever so much for all your kindness and consideration for me; and please don't make too much of my humble services; it was quite a pleasure to wait upon you—and—and——" Here she broke down, for, in spite of her rigid training, she was only human, and, indeed, very young.

"There, there," Carruthers said soothingly, "you're a dear, kind little thing; and I am very fond of you, as well as grateful for your kindness and attention to me, but, you know, the best of friends must part. If you are ever in trouble and need the sympathy and help of a friend, let me know."

"I thank you from the bottom of my heart, Sir Ashleigh," replied the nurse, looking frankly into the steady, honest eyes of Carruthers; "and, if anything further should happen in connection with that fearful creature, pray let me know."

"I will, I will, I promise you that," said Carruthers; "and, now, farewell!"

Then an irresistible impulse moved him; he lowered his head and kissed Nurse Everest on the cheek.

"Oh, Sir Ashleigh," she exclaimed, blushing deeply at first, then trembling from head to foot and turning deadly pale. "You shouldn't have done that, indeed; you should not!"

"You are right; I was a brute; and I beg your pardon! I am too impulsive; but it came from my heart; and I will not offend again."

As he said this he coloured deeply, grasped his stick, and hurried from the room and the hotel into the street.

As he walked slowly towards the open country, he thought; "What a nice, sweet, modest girl she is! She speaks the King's English, too, like a lady; and I am certain she is one. At any rate she comes from a good, healthy stock; there can be no possible doubt on that score. . . . I hope I didn't go too far! Just like me; brute that I am! . . . By Jove, it wouldn't be safe for me to see too much of her! . . . I should soon be very fond of her, and it wouldn't be fair either. . . . Yet, after all, how infinitely superior a woman like that would be as a wife, compared to those selfish, worldly, vain butterflies of fashion, born. and bred in frivolity, and living in an atmosphere of artificiality and untruth! Women with no higher aims than to outdo each other in dress and to madly rush from one excitement to another! . . . It seems to me that their religion is humbug; their friendship is humbug; and the greatest humbug of all-their so-called love! Yet these are the destined mothers of our coming race. It is too dreadful to contemplate!"

As Carruthers walked along thinking deeply, he saw approaching him the police inspector, Mr. Jones, who saluted him, and said:

"Sir Ashleigh, I should be glad to speak to you for a few minutes."

"Certainly. We can stroll together up this quiet lane. Well, how have you succeeded in your pursuit of the woman?"

"I think we are at last on the right track, Sir Ashleigh. Yes, there can be no doubt of it. The criminal has been caught red-handed at last."

"Indeed, are you sure?" inquired Carruthers, excitedly. "Describe her!"

The police inspector, before replying, gave Carruthers a keen glance, then said with a smile:

"So you have already made up your mind that the offender is a woman?"

Carruthers realised in an instant that he had given himself away; but replied with sufficient self-possession, "Well, of course, I had my own opinion on the matter; but never mind that; tell me what she was like. Give me the minutest description to enable me to confirm my views or destroy them."

As a matter of course, Carruthers fully expected to hear the criminal described as a beautiful woman, with white face, black luxuriant hair, and blood-red lips. He was, however, doomed to disappointment. The woman portrayed by the police inspector was an old, hideous, decrepit hag, nearly bent double; with yellow, wrinkled parchment skin and nearly toothless.

"Indeed," exclaimed Carruthers. "Well, I confess that is not the description I expected to hear; but no matter. Tell me how the capture was effected."

"Well, Sir Ashleigh, it was like this, and all along of the Society for the Prevention of Cruelty to Children. One of their people was passing at night by a cottage near the village of ———, a terrible, lonely, out-of-the-way place, notorious for drunkards, wife-beaters, and starving children, when he heard a cry which seemed to be that of a child in great agony. Being aware of the cruelty to children which prevailed there, the man rushed to the hovel, and finding the door open, entered. The man who lived there and his wife were both in a drunken sleep. He then looked into the little back room, and there, in a crib, he saw the bleeding body of a child of two, and, bending over it, stood a hideous old crone, dressed in black, and nearly bent double with age—who (would you believe it?) had made her few remaining teeth meet in the child's throat, and was intent on sucking its blood, just as a wolf might do to a lamb. She did not hear the steps of the man, being too absorbed by her gruesome meal, and took no heed whatever until his hand grasped her. Then, however, she struggled like a fiend. It required all the man's strength—and, fortunately, he was very powerfully built—to secure her. He succeeded in time, and handed her over to us—and now, Sir Ashleigh, she's safe in a strong cell. Lord, when we put the bracelets on, there was blood on the corners of her mouth, and also on her black dress—which, mind you, was made of real good stuff, such as a lady might wear; not by no manner of means the rags of a tramp."

"Ha!" exclaimed Carruthers, as if a sudden light had flashed upon his mind. "How long has she been in custody?"

"Only since last night, Sir Ashleigh. She's safe enough now at any rate. Would you like to see her? If so I can admit you into her cell."

"Willingly," said Carruthers, "that is er—er—look here, Inspector, I'll have a look at her, if you like; but I don't want my name to be mixed up in the matter. I am known in this district, and object to have my name in any way connected with the affair. I may know more about the business than I can say; but, please, not a word about me! Do you understand? It will be enough if she is convicted on this last charge alone."

"Very well, Sir Ashleigh, I quite understand. We are accustomed to keep things dark."

"All right, then. Now conduct me to the woman's cell."

...

CHAPTER XVIII

CARRUTHERS VISITS
THE WOMAN IN BLACK

◎

When the inspector and Carruthers entered the cell, a female dressed in black was sitting on the edge of a pallet bed, with her elbows on her knees, and her face in her hands. She looked up when the two men entered; rose to her feet and faced them, standing proudly erect with her arms crossed on her chest. The expression of scorn was, however, mixed with fear.

"Hullo!" exclaimed Inspector Jones, who was a stout, red-faced, snub-nosed man, with mutton chop whiskers, and a low, gruff voice; "What does this mean? There must be some mistake. This can't be the same woman as I turned the key on last night!" Then he added in a whisper to Carruthers: "This woman stands upright, and looks only forty, while the prisoner as I locked up last night was bent double with age, and looked, at least, a hundred."

Although these words were whispered into the ear of Sir Ashleigh, they were distinctly heard by the woman, whose sense of hearing must have been supernaturally acute; and she immediately gathered courage from them. Turning to Inspector Jones, with a face expressing hatred and contempt, she said:

"Oh, indeed, so you have found out your preposterous mistake at last! I knew you would. Do I look like the decrepit old crone that slipped through your clumsy fingers last night, at the very moment I happened to be passing?"

Inspector Jones was staggered for a time; in fact, almost hypnotised by the intensity of her gaze; but he soon mastered himself, and said:

"Come, come, my beauty, that won't wash! How do you account for the blood upon your dress, eh?"

"I expected you would say that," she replied; "and I admit circumstances are against me; but, in spite of that, I am innocent. I will explain it all to you. I, too, heard the infant's cry, and rushed to save it, and as I did so the hag you mentioned tore past me and escaped. I was in an agony of grief at the sight of the cruelly murdered child, for I love children dearly, and I threw myself upon the corpse and tenderly kissed its lips; and in doing this both my face and dress were stained with blood. Yes, I can solemnly assure you that this is how the mistake occurred. You seized me, an innocent woman, and let the guilty one escape."

Inspector Jones glanced at Carruthers to ascertain from his expression of countenance what he thought of this explanation; but his stern, hard-set face convinced him that his companion was not taken in by the not very plausible story, and he said: "Won't wash yet. I had you fast enough, I know; and I'm not in the habit of letting my prisoners slip through my fingers, so you don't come over me by gammon of that sort. If you looked older last night than you do today, it may be because of the way you doubled yourself up to avoid recognition or some other pretty little game; but you're the same woman; and that's the point."

"She is," said Carruthers, with deep conviction.

"Ashleigh, dear Ashleigh!" said the woman, in appealing, pathetic tones, and with tears in her eyes, "surely you will not allow yourself to be led away by this base man's assertion! You of all people in the world, and after all that has passed between us. This poor man is to be excused on account of his ignorance; indeed, everyone is apt to make mistakes.

But you, Ashleigh, you who have known me so long and so intimately! No, no, I cannot believe it! You whom I have trusted so deeply; you could never, with your kind heart, betray a helpless woman!" Here she threw herself on her knees, before him, extending her arms, while the tears fell from her eyes.

With all his courage and energy Carruthers was emotional; and this appeal hit him hard. He was deeply moved in spite of his better sense; and he felt a lump rise in his throat. She looked beautiful in her admirably acted character of an innocent victim of circumstances, and Carruthers noticed that even the inspector was touched; but this made Ashleigh pull himself together, for he rightly thought that if both made fools of themselves, the woman would escape. So he said, in a firm voice: "No, base creature, I will do nothing whatever to save you! You cannot deceive me by plausible lies. I now know your past life, and if I choose I could tell many things you imagine to be unknown. You look incredulous, but the proofs are in my hands. So far as I am concerned you shall suffer all that the law can inflict on you for your crimes, especially for the murder of the innocent child last night!"

At these words, the creature rose from her knees, clutched at her bosom, and shrank away from Carruthers, with looks of malignant hatred. After a pause of a few moments, she said, with a forced and mocking laugh: "Oh, I perfectly understand, Sir Ashleigh Carruthers! You who took advantage of my innocence under a false name and promised to marry me. Yes, I know your true character at last! It was, indeed, a worthy, gentlemanly action, to take advantage of a poor girl, to delude her trusting innocence, ruin her, and, then, cast her off for ever. O, man! man! thou arch traitor to our too confiding sex! . . . Oh, God! how can hearts be so hard?" Here she rose to a really fine melodramatic frenzy. Carruthers was nearly beside himself with rage and indignation, and burst out in protest:

"You lie, lie basely, fiendish creature" Say, did I ever meet you more than once, and even then by chance! What! for a few words of passing gallantry, imprudently provoked by yourself, which I have since bitterly repented, must I be dragged into the abyss of your vile, unnatural life? I warn you not to provoke me into the exposure of your abominable past; but if you dare to mix me up with your vile life, I will tell all I know!" Then turning to the astonished inspector, he said, "Let us go!"

•••

CHAPTER XIX

INSPECTOR JONES READS
MR. WALDEGRAVE'S STORY

◯

"Jones," said Carruthers, as the two left the prison cell behind them, and stepped into the street, which led to the Abbot's Hotel, "not one word of that woman's wild story was true, I assure you!"

"I can well believe that, Sir Ashleigh. We of the force are used to tarradiddles."

"Listen to me," said Carruthers; "all she said might appear plausible enough from the manner in which she played her part. But I can assure you, on my word of honour as a gentleman, that I never met that woman but once in my life. It was, in fact, in church; and I soon after encountered her in a place where she had taken shelter from the rain, and there I spoke to her. We then walked together nearly to the hotel. It is not true that I ruined her under a promise of marriage, and in an assumed name. I gave no name at all, neither did I know hers. She must have found out my name, and you heard the use she made of it."

"Nothing more likely, Sir Ashleigh."

"Only a few gallantries passed between us, and with that exception, her whole tale is an utter fabrication," said Carruthers.

"Of that I am quite convinced," said Jones.

"Now, listen to me again, inspector. You have to do with a most extraordinary, not to say supernatural, case. You, in the discharge of your useful calling, have been used to deal with all sorts and conditions of men, and, harder still, women, but you never had to do with a case at all like the present, and if I am not mistaken, you will never encounter such another."

"Yet I've come across some rum ones in my time," observed Jones, with a self-satisfied air.

"Whatever experiences you may have had, and I've no doubt they have been valuable and interesting, compared with the present case, have been merely commonplace; while this is unprecedented," insisted Carruthers.

The inspector now became deeply interested, and he looked at Carruthers very keenly. The latter, observing this, suddenly stopped and stood in front of Jones, fixing him with his eye, and said in a low, earnest tone: "Please to remember that what I am about to say must be kept as secret as the grave."

"Mum's the word, Sir Ashleigh."

"Jones," said Carruthers, "do you believe in witchcraft?"

A fatuous smile broke over the red, commonplace face of the policeman, and Carruthers, who noticed it, and clearly read its meaning, added: "I don't care whether you do or do not; I didn't myself a few days ago; but since I have known that woman——"

Here Inspector Jones turned suddenly upon the speaker with such a scrutinising and suspicious look on his round red face, and in his little round, blue eyes, which, we may add, were rather close together, that Carruthers broke off in his sentence and said: "Oh, I can easily read the thoughts that are passing through your brain, inspector! You are thinking that probably my mind has become unhinged as a consequence of my late illness; that I am slightly insane, in fact. Now, tell me frankly, is not that the truth?"

Jones coloured slightly and looked down at his well-polished bluchers. "Well, well," said Carruthers; "it is quite natural that you should think so; and I do not blame you. It is part of your profession to be suspicious; but you shall follow me back to the hotel; and I will give you a manuscript to read, from which, I think you will see that there are ample reasons in support of my belief in witchcraft."

When they reached the hotel, Jones followed Carruthers to his room. Nurse Everest had gone when they entered.

"Sit down, Jones, in that easy chair; smoke if you like—here's tobacco."

"Thanks, Sir Ashleigh," and Jones drew from his pocket a clay pipe, which he carefully filled, after seating himself.

"This is the manuscript I spoke of; but before you read, it would be, perhaps, advisable that I should tell you how it came into my hands. It is just over a week ago since I returned to this district from South Africa. My home is at Tudor Hall, near ———. I had received an invitation to visit an old college friend, who had lately married, as soon as I returned to England. I took the train one Sunday morning, and, in time, arrived at the lodge gate. The woman in charge informed me that my friend was still abroad, and his return uncertain. I left the place, and instead of returning home, set out on a fifteen miles' walk to Abbotswood, where some friends of mine used to live. About a mile or two from this place is the old church of St. Cuthbert's. When I reached the churchyard it was getting dark, and as the evening service was going on, I resolved to go in and rest. I took my seat in an empty pew near the door. A violent storm began at that moment, and suddenly I became aware that a lady was in the same pew as myself. She was, I noticed, very young and extremely beautiful, and was dressed entirely in black. As she was without a hymn-book, I lent her the one I found in front of me, and we shared it. As she returned it, I again noticed her uncommon and exquisite beauty, and made up my mind to follow her at the end of the service. Then the late vicar of St. Cuthbert's, whom I had known in my youth, and who had been a great friend of my late father, gave out the text of his sermon; and, as he did so, he happened to look round and fixed his eyes first on me, and after, on the lady near me. Then, to my astonishment, he suddenly became very pale, his eyes fixed in a stony stare, he trembled from head to foot, was seized with fainting, and fell on the floor of the pulpit. He was carried out of the church, took to his bed, from which he never rose again. Before his death, he expressed an earnest wish to see me. As you are aware, I was laid up at the same time; and Dr. Leach attended us both. When I was sufficiently well to go out, which happened to be the very day Mr. Waldegrave died, I went, in company with Dr. Leach, to see him. He greeted me very kindly, placed the manuscript I have just given you in my hands, and, after a few words, died. Do me the favour of reading it. I have some letters to write, and, therefore, shall not disturb you."

Inspector Jones commenced the strange story of the Woman in Black, while Carruthers began a long letter to Nurse Everest, informing her of the capture of the creature; and, in addition, giving an account of meeting her in the police station cell, in the presence of the inspector.

During this time Jones was absorbed in the late vicar's story, frowning now and again; and puffing with great vigour at his short pipe.

He was so astonished occasionally that he was compelled to pause for some minutes, during which time he wrinkled his brow, pursed his lips, and looked altogether like a man out of his depth.

Not a word was spoken by either, until Jones folded the papers, placed them on the table, and uttered a deep sigh.

"Well, inspector, what do you make of it all, eh?"

"Well, Sir Ashleigh, to be frank, I don't know what to make of it. I suppose there's no doubt as the old gentleman was right in his mind when he wrote what he did; and, seeing it's dated some years back, it must have been quite his opinion and belief; and I must admit that I knew the old vicar myself and I always found him a very kind, sensible old gentleman of irreproachable lite, who would not willingly and knowingly deceive or injure anybody."

"In fact, you are not now surprised at the conclusion I have been compelled to arrive at, eh, Jones?"

"Well, Sir Ashleigh, if all this story is strictly true, and the man who wrote it was sound in his mind, I must confess that I am not surprised at your opinion. For myself, as a humble member of the force, I would rather not give any opinion on the matter, but await, with eyes and ears wide open, the course of events."

• • •

CHAPTER XX

CARRUTHERS RETURNS
TO TUDOR HALL

◯

Sir Ashleigh Carruthers returned to Tudor Hall on the following day. As the train did not leave Abbotswood until mid-day, he called on Inspector Jones before starting. After some talk together, Carruthers said:

"You are doubtless surprised that the woman you arrested should have appeared so much younger the day after, when we visited the cell?"

"I was indeed, Sir Ashleigh; it was quite beyond belief."

"Well, inspector, do you know that I have seen her appear younger still; in fact, when I first met her, she appeared to be between eighteen and twenty years of age."

Jones opened his eyes as widely as possible when he heard this apparently preposterous statement. Could, he thought, it be possible for the same woman to appear over eighty and eighteen!

Carruthers, in response to the look of astonishment, mixed with incredulity, that appeared on the inspector's face, added: "My statement is perfectly true; and what is more, if you keep her under lock and key long enough, and feed her on prison fare, which, however, I feel quite certain she will not touch, you will find that she will shrivel up and become an almost toothless old hag again. Take care of yourself, for she will fly at the throat of any person entering her cell; that is my warning to you. She lives only on human blood; without it she dies; with it, she may live on for unnumbered years."

"Well, Sir Ashleigh, if that is true; she is a wonderful creature; and, as you said, I certainly never did meet with such a case before!"

"There is another thing I want to say to you; I mean about the ring. Never for one moment forget that it is a magic ring; and it is entirely owing to the loss of it that her capture was effected. Had it been in her possession all attempts to secure her would have failed. The ring enables her to make herself invisible at will; it has enabled her to live on heaven knows how many years, and to defy all attacks! Without it she is powerless. So, let me solemnly warn you by all possible means, to keep the ring out of her sight and possession."

Inspector Jones smiled a self-satisfied smile, and said: "She's not likely to get it, Sir Ashleigh, not if I know it! I have it safe in my possession; and I have had it examined by a big professor at the British Museum, and he says it is ancient Egyptian; and the inscription in hieroglyphics proves it to have once belonged to a priest of high rank, and that it was probably taken from his mummy."

"Another strange confirmation!" exclaimed Carruthers. He then told Jones the dream of Nurse Everest in reference to the Woman in Black, and her wild despair at the loss of the ring. Soon after this Carruthers left the police station in order to be in time for his train; after asking Jones to keep him well informed as to what happened to his strange prisoner, about whose safe custody he could not help feeling rather nervous.

On reaching Tudor Hall, Carruthers found that the workmen had not over-exerted themselves in carrying out his directions during his absence. Many inquiries had been made about his health, for reports had been rife that his wound had re-opened; and many of his neighbours and acquaintances appeared to have felt genuine interest and sympathy. Domestic duties and estate accounts kept him busy for some time; and neighbours called to congratulate him on his recovery and to hear from his own lips an account of his illness. He soon learnt, to his deep annoyance, that what he feared had happened; a garbled account of the Woman in Black had appeared in the local papers, in spite of the reticence of Inspector Jones and Nurse Everest; and, of course, his name appeared in a way that delighted the lovers of scandal. This resulted in Carruthers being treated very coldly by many of his straight-laced acquaintances. Some match-making mammas, who had boldly angled for Sir Ashleigh as a husband for one or other of their dear darlings, now denounced him to their sympathising female friends.

On the whole, Carruthers was not sorry to miss the society of some of the respectable bores whose inane talk had so annoyed him. He had quite enough little worries he could not avoid, such as letters for subscriptions from persons in distant parishes for the building of some new church, circulars from enterprising tradesmen touting their wares, money lenders offering him money—the strictest secrecy observed, and begging letters from all parts of the kingdom. Then there were legal complications due to petty misunderstandings about the paltriest matters; bills to be paid, and accounts to be kept, and visits from people he cared nothing for, which, unfortunately, he felt he was bound to return. All this, together with bothers with the builders and stupidities of the workmen, often made him long for the wild veldt with its exciting adventures, and the genial society of his brother officers. It was during this period of dull, monotonous existence, the humdrum, prosaic life of the mere Philistine, that Carruthers began to lament the loneliness of his life. He thought as he sat in his smoking den, with a cigar between his lips: "Why, the poorest and humblest have someone to share trouble and pleasure with!" . . . Was it his own fault that he had no one? . . . "Perhaps . . . but I am not to be caught by those who openly angle for me. . . . No; I am determined to make my own choice, in my own way, and at my own time."

All that we have said about the state of Carruthers' feelings will prove to the thoughtful reader that he missed the tender tact, the sweet voice, and gentle, truthful countenance and soothing presence of Nurse Everest. He did not himself yet know the truth; but circumstances would in time make him fully acknowledge it.

• • •

CHAPTER XXI
NURSE EVEREST
IN LONDON

N urse Everest had hardly resettled herself in her room in London, after leaving Abbotswood, when a voluminous letter reached her in a writing she did not know. She looked at the post-mark, and, on reading it, a thrill ran through her. On tearing open the envelope she searched for the signature; and looked with delight at the firm, strong writing in which Carruthers' name appeared. What could he have to communicate so soon after her departure? The letter began with—"Dear Nurse Everest." Well, that was simple enough; he could hardly have addressed her in any other manner. In spite of that wise reflection, she could not help her heart beating. There was nothing compromising in the substance of the letter; it might have come from any other grateful patient, for she had been accustomed to expressions of gratitude, both verbal and written; but there was something in the personality and bearing of Carruthers; and, in addition, the mystery which enveloped his case, which were all pre-eminently calculated to captivate a woman of the imaginative temperament of Nurse Everest; more especially when we consider that that portion of her nature had been nearly starved. She was half angry with herself for her weakness and softness of heart. What could a man of his social position and fortune have in common with herself? Undoubtedly the best thing she could do was to forget him, and yet she felt she could not succeed in banishing him from her heart; his image would obtrude itself when she was unoccupied for a moment; and her struggles to banish it were all in vain.

On her return, Nurse Everest had been questioned by the other nurses about the case she had been concerned in, as was the usual custom; although this was forbidden by the matron when they met at meal time. Of course, she only spoke of the medical aspect of the case. Some of the women, however, noticed a change in her tone and manner: she was reserved and quiet, and often appeared to be lost in thought.

Women are quick to notice changes of this kind, and those who had been most intimate with her resented her want of confidence and change of tone. Then they thought of the thick letter with the Abbotswood postmark, and when she told them that its contents did not refer to the case, they, with the rapidity of female minds, concluded that it was a love letter, and taxed Nurse Everest with being in love with her late patient. At this direct charge, delivered with a bluntness characteristic of many women, Nurse Everest's face and neck were suffused with burning blushes, while tears of shame rose to her blue grey eyes.

We need not describe the delight of her tormentors at the successful result of their attack or describe the silly and rude jokes they made about wedding cakes, bridesmaids, and orange blossoms; they were of the usual contemptible kind.

After an internal struggle, Nurse Everest adopted the only wise policy possible—she appeared to enter into the fun and to enjoy the rude attempts at wit. This produced the desired result, the women tired of their chaff, and were soon discussing interesting cases. When she was alone in her little room, away from the cackle and gibes of her unsympathetic companions, she could indulge in those dreams and aspirations so dear, and perhaps, so necessary to the young, but for which so many have no sympathy. Poor girl! She was forlorn indeed! Yet the very hopelessness of her case did not make her desire that she had never loved;

on the contrary, she felt it something to be able to give her warm heart to someone whom she felt was not unworthy of it, and, indeed, agreed with the poet:

> 'Twere better to have loved and lost
> Than never to have loved at all.

In her unselfishness she blamed herself alone, and not as so many women would have done, the man who had won her heart in spite of herself. It was not his fault that she had fallen in love with him. With her it had almost been love at first sight. She loved him, not because he had tried to win her, but almost because he had done nothing of the kind—in fact, she loved him because he was himself. She had soon felt it necessary to attempt to stifle the affection so soon awakened within her, and she fervently hoped she had never by word or look manifested it. It appeared to her that to be permitted to love Carruthers secretly—to worship his image enshrined within her heart—was happiness.

She was quite willing to let

> Concealment, like a worm i' the bud, feed
> on her damask cheek.

And this state of feeling continued from day to day, week to week, and from month to month; and Nurse Everest's existence was a dream of love, which, however, did not prevent her performing satisfactorily her daily routine duties.

As the reader has doubtless guessed, Nurse Everest had been born and educated a lady. Her father had been a colonel in the Army, who had been killed in the Soudan. His widow, finding herself in very reduced circumstances, had been obliged to remove her daughter, Celia, from an expensive school at Windsor, where her late father, Colonel Macullum, had placed her with the object of giving her every possible educational advantage. His untimely death, in the service of his country, cut short her acquirement of numerous showy accomplishments, and her mother, with great good sense, decided that henceforth her training should be of a more domestic and practical kind. Celia took a great interest in her new pursuits, and developed much skill in nursing the sick in the village to which she and her mother had retired. About a year after Colonel Macullum's death his widow passed away, and Celia was left alone, face to face with the necessity of earning her own living. During her benevolent labours amongst the poor and suffering, she had made the acquaintance of a hospital nurse, who appreciated her talent and determination. Enough money had been left her to enable Celia Macullum to go through the necessary training; and, at an early age, she had passed, with signal success, all the required examinations, and entered a home from which she could be called upon to attend private cases. Her personal charm had caused many medical students to propose to her, all of whom she had, without hesitation, refused. Nothing could have induced her to marry without real love.

Nurse Everest also disliked silly flirtations; her womanly dignity sheltered her from vulgar folly of the kind, and she was naturally looked upon by her companions as a pretty girl destined to be an old maid. This reserve on her part had aroused intense interest in the letter from Abbotswood; and accounted for the banter of her fellow nurses.

The relations of Colonel Macullum had been very indignant with him because his marriage had been founded on love, and not on worldly interest or pride, and the result had been that none of them had taken any further interest in him; or, after his death, in his widow and only child.

Nurse Everest had really been afraid that some of the family might out of charity, hearing of her double bereavement, have offered her assistance, and tried to take her from the position of useful independence she had so courageously chosen.

Had she known more of the world she might have been aware that penniless orphans are not, as a rule, searched for as coveted treasures. But in order to elude any search that she thought might be made for her, she had assumed the name of Everest; and although without the sympathy of real friends or the affection of any relation, she was happy in the conscientious discharge of her important duties; and was rewarded by that glow in the heart which independence and self-respect can alone inspire.

• • •

CHAPTER XXII

INSPECTOR JONES'S ENCOUNTER WITH THE WOMAN IN BLACK

◊

We must now return to Inspector Jones, after Sir Ashleigh Carruthers had left him. He was deeply impressed with what he had been told, about the mysterious power of the ring, and the confirmation, by a dream, of the opinion of the professor at the British Museum on the subject. Jones thought so much that his head began to ache—thinking not being his strong point—and he resolved to take a walk through a neighbouring wood in order to readjust his scattered ideas. Inspector Jones was not prone by temperament to superstitious opinions, or belief in the occult. On the contrary, in his experience as a policeman he had seen so much apparent mystery and cunning quackery exposed and rendered ridiculous that he had very naturally become a thorough sceptic. As we have pretty nearly indicated, Jones was not overburdened with brains, but he had the natural instincts of the sleuth-hound, and in addition, the tenacity of the bull-dog. Neither was Jones without tact of a certain kind; he knew admirably when to hold his tongue and wait patiently for developments; he was also possessed of great firmness and decision of character; and these qualities fitted him for the position he held at Abbotswood. As we have said before, he was a man of splendid physique, had rather a bullet head, very florid complexion, mutton-chop whiskers, a strong, deep voice, short dark hair, and, indeed, was a man of strong will, honest as the day, and afraid of nothing.

Jones was not a man to be trifled with, because his courage was dauntless, his sense of duty inflexible, and his word his bond. His main faults were his entire confidence in his own qualities, and his disregard of anything outside his own limited knowledge and experience. What he did not know, he tacitly thought hardly worth knowing. As he wandered through the wood paths, lost in deep thought, he found considerable difficulty in reconciling the strange story of Carruthers, told in such evident good faith, with his own experience and theory of life. He scouted the idea of the supernatural as absurd and impossible. Whatever appeared on the surface to be occult or supernatural was, in reality, nothing but a more or less clever piece of trickery, and a detective like himself was the man born to expose it. Inspector Jones admitted that there were mysteries, or, rather, apparent mysteries, in nature; but it was only because we did not understand the *modus operandi*. He reasoned thus with himself.

"Sir Ashleigh Carruthers was a gentleman of position and wealth, and quite incapable of playing off upon him any practical joke. He had no object in deceiving him in any way. Then, again, he was a well-educated man, and apparently no fool. . . . Yet, strange to say, he believed in the supernatural, which was, of course, impossible. . . . therefore, he must be mistaken. . . . His good faith was beyond question; but might he not be naturally superstitious, and, constantly, prone to give credence to reports from unreliable persons and sources? . . . Yes, that must be the solution of the mystery!" Jones's face cleared up and his brow smoothed itself; but, after a moment's thought, his countenance darkened again with doubt. . . . "Ah, but the manuscript story! What about that? Surely the late Vicar of St. Cuthbert's, a thoughtful good man of quite blameless life, would not have willingly made up such a story if he had thought it false; and then consigned it to Sir Ashleigh Carruthers on his death-bed, and almost with his last breath! . . . Was he, too, deceived? . . . Besides, had not he himself been witness of the wonderful transformation of his prisoner from a decrepit old hag to a comparatively young woman! . . . Could that be explained by natural laws? Might it not possibly be clever acting on her part? Then how about the wonderful power of the ring?" Then a thought struck the inspector, and his face assumed a determined look. "I will try her with it!" He had the ring locked up in his own iron safe at the station. "Yes, I will see what effect the sight of it produces on her!"

Then he remembered what Carruthers had told him about the result of her being kept without her only food, blood! and that deprived of that she would shrink and shrivel into the condition that she had at first presented when arrested. Jones did not think for a moment of his own personal peril if he entered the cell when the creature was mad with famine. The idea of any human creature, especially a woman, daring to attack him was too absurd for a moment's consideration. The truth or falsehood of the change in the woman wrought by want of food was something solid to base an opinion on; and Inspector Jones started off at once to possess himself of the ring and face the woman with it. He had not seen his prisoner that day, and tomorrow she was to be removed to the county prison to await her trial for the murder of the child.

Full of his new idea he hastened his steps to the police station, and was soon in his room. He opened his locked safe, placed the ring in a breast pocket, and entered the cell. There, to his utter astonishment, he saw the woman crouching on the floor near her low bed, and looking as old and decrepit as on the night when he first turned the key upon her. "Well, I'm——!" He did not finish his sentence; but stood with eyes and mouth open to their fullest extent, lost in wonder.

The old hag looked at him with a fiendish expression in her black eyes, in which all her remaining vitality appeared to be concentrated, and said in a penetrating, guttural whisper:

"So you have come at last to gloat and triumph over the unmerited misfortunes of a poor, suffering woman? That's manly, very manly, isn't it?"

"Humph!" grunted Jones, ignoring the reproach. "So we're shriv-elling up, are we? That seems to be a favourite trick of yours; and you do it very well, too, I admit. Well, it's your own fault if you refuse to eat the usual prison fare! Mind, you'll get no other!"

"Fool!" screamed the hag as loudly as she could. "You know me not! You are a contemptible coward after all, in spite of your huge bulk! Give me back my ring, you villain! The ring you basely stole from me! I know you have it on you. I feel its influence emanate from you!"

"Your what? Did you say your ring?" exclaimed Jones, in feigned astonishment. "Now, if you had asked for a tender, juicy rump steak and a pint of porter I shouldn't have blamed you—not that you'd have got it either; but a ring! What on earth can a woman of your condition want with a ring?" Jones's small eyes twinkled with amusement as he thus chaffed his apparently helpless victim.

"Give it me, give it me, you ugly mountain of flesh; or I will wrest it from you with these hands!" she exclaimed.

"Indeed," exclaimed Jones, with an amused expression on his red, round face. "I think not much! Now, look here, what would you say if I were to show you a pretty little toy that I bought at a fair only the other day?" he said, coolly, enjoying her impotent fury. "Let me see if I can find it. . . . Yes, here it is!" and, taking the ring from his inside breast pocket, he deliberately attempted to put it on his little finger, which, by-the-bye, was a big one. He could only succeed in balancing it on the tip.

At this the frenzy of the woman was roused to the highest point, and she screamed out: "Villain! miscreant! Give me the ring, or dread the worst! I tell you, idiot, the terrible gods of Egypt who guard that ring are even now standing behind you" They have delivered you into my hands. Give it me without delay, or——"

"Now, here is a pretty, a very pretty thing; and what shall be done to the owner of this very pretty thing?" demanded the inspector in his most jocular manner. The hag's fury became boundless and uncontrol-lable, as Jones flashed the ring before her eyes, balanced on the tip of the little finger of his huge hand. As he moved his hand, as ill-luck would have it, the ring fell to the floor of the cell. With the lightning speed of a cat pouncing on a mouse, the hag had seized it and placed it on her finger, before the giant Jones could bend his big body to wrest it from her clutches; and, worse still, had flown at his throat and fastened her fangs there, ere he could make the slightest attempt at resistance.

Jones was taken completely by surprise, and was, indeed, thrown off his balance; his foot slipped, and in an instant, the colossus had measured his gigantic length on the floor, the back of his bead, as it struck the ground, sounding like an empty cask. For a few moments he remained stunned; but his thick head saved him. Meanwhile the woman vampire held on to her prey like a terrier to a rat, oblivious of everything but the unspeakable delight she derived from the indulgence of her abominable appetite. Her victim was so entirely in her power that for a time he was quite incapable of making any resistance. It is needless to say that he soon made every possible effort to free himself; but his strength was so enfeebled by the loss of blood that he could barely move his head from side to side. The meal was a long one; but, fortunately, at last the creature was gorged to repletion, and fell back sound asleep on the floor of the cell, like a vulture glutted with carrion.

• • •

CHAPTER XXIII
ILLNESS OF JONES

The first intimation of alarm as to the condition of Inspector Jones was given by a thin stream of blood issuing from the prison cell, which was seen by one of the men, who, on opening the door, found him in the unconscious condition we described in the last chapter. Close to Jones, also lying on the floor, fast asleep, was the woman prisoner. At the first glance the man thought both were dead, and was greatly astonished and puzzled to account for the fact. The man called loudly for assistance; and with the help of two other officers the heavy body of Jones was carefully removed to his own room; a fourth man was sent for Dr. Leach, who, on his arrival, ordered the inspector to be removed to his own home. There he was received by Mrs. Jones, with every mark of concern and affection. When the still insensible man had been placed on his bed, Dr. Leach carefully examined the wounds in his throat; and, without hesitation, pronounced them to be precisely identical with those inflicted on Sir Ashleigh Carruthers and on several other patients whom he had attended. He ordered similar treatment to that he had directed before; and took his leave after impressing on Mrs. Jones that her husband would require the most careful and unremitting attention, as it was a very dangerous case from the excessive loss of blood; and that, in fact, he considered his life was in great danger.

We can imagine the consternation of the wife, who adored her husband, and had a family of six children, at this plain speaking of the doctor. Like a true and devoted woman, however, she carried out, in the most careful manner, the directions given her, and was rewarded, in a few days, by seeing a marked change for the better in the condition of her husband. The recovery of inspector Jones from the terrible attack made upon him by the Woman in Black was very slow; but, owing partly to his splendid physique and constitution, not forgetting the unsleeping vigilance of his devoted wife, and the care and skill of Dr. Leach, the head of the police at Abbotswood in time was restored to sufficient health and strength to enable him to resume his accustomed duties.

• • •

CHAPTER XXIV

ESCAPE OF
THE WOMAN IN BLACK

W e must now return to the Woman in Black. Strange as it may appear, in spite of the care with which he had been guarded, it is nevertheless true that the evil creature had managed to elude her captors, and was now, unfortunately, at large again. It was quite impossible to hide the unpleasant truth, much as the police desired to keep the matter, which reflected discredit on themselves, secret.

"What was the good of the police if they allowed such a dangerous and notorious criminal to escape?"

That was what the public would naturally inquire. Each member of the force was inclined to cast the blame on the other. Having no better way to explain the mystery, they agreed on saying that their concern for the condition of their chief caused them to forget the prisoner, who, taking advantage of the opportunity, had escaped during the excitement.

Of course, it was very culpable neglect on their part, they admitted; but it could not be helped, and the least said about the matter the better. This easy-going philosophy did not succeed, however, and before long the local papers issued flaming placards to the following effect:

CAPTURE OF THE WOMAN IN BLACK.
MURDEROUS ATTACK ON INSPECTOR JONES BY THE PRISONER.

HER MIRACULOUS ESCAPE THROUGH LOCKED DOORS.
CRITICAL CONDITION OF INSPECTOR JONES.
EXTRAORDINARY REVELATIONS: UNHEARD-OF CRIMES.

The sale of local papers, spiced in this manner, was immense, for the people of Abbotswood and the surrounding country, like those of Athens, spent their time in hearing or relating some new thing.

Now, Carruthers did not take in the local papers, but an attentive friend sent him a copy of the one referred to, and asked his opinion of it. He wrote to his friend that he was very interested in the strange case, that it ought to be most carefully inquired into, but he gave no word or hint that Jones's experience had any bearing on his own case. Although he wrote in this cool way to the sender of the paper, Carruthers was very excited about the matter, and at once made up his mind to visit Inspector Jones, and hear the full account of the case from his own lips. He took the train to Abbotswood, and was soon at Jones's door.

Mrs. Jones presented herself, and on Carruthers telling her his name, and that he desired to see her husband, he was at once asked to walk in, and, after a few minutes' delay, was taken to the bedside of the sick man. Jones, whose face had lost all colour, and was thin and drawn, greeted his visitor with the ghost of his former genial smile, and soon told, in a feeble voice, the story of his extraordinary experience.

"Ha!" exclaimed Carruthers, when Jones had finished, "it is a very remarkable affair; but you remember I warned you to take care of yourself, and not to show the ring."

"Yes, Sir Ashleigh, but who ever could foresee such an attack as that? It passes all belief. Why, I can hardly believe it now! I was so taken aback that my foot slipped, and down I came such a cropper on the back of my head that I lost all consciousness."

"There, there," broke in Carruthers, "don't excite yourself by talking too much. You are evidently very weak." But Jones liked to have his say, and proceeded:

"Then, Sir Ashleigh, the escape of the prisoner! There, that beats me! She's a witch, that's what she is; there's no doubt about it!"

"So you have come round at last to my opinion," said Carruthers. "You'll never laugh at witchcraft again, I am certain."

"No, by heavens! I never will," exclaimed Jones, bringing his big bony fist down on the table beside him with all the force he could muster.

Carruthers laughed gaily, and, after many kindly expressions of sympathy, shook the inspector's hand and departed.

On his way back to the station, Carruthers muttered to himself: "It is lucky that I called on Jones and heard his version of the story. He would never have told so much to any outsider, I know. More links in the chain; and how well they all fit together! I see it all clearly now. The ring is at the bottom of the mystery. If we could only get that, we could defy all her machinations. How strange, too, that an ordinary police inspector should talk about the gods of Egypt haunting him in his sleep all the time he had possession of the ring. The hawk-headed deity, Horus, the one with the cat's head—that was "Pasht"; another, with the crocodile's head, was Sebek; and the bull, Apis. How accurately he described all of them! Ah, Ashleigh, my boy, there are more wonders and fathomless mysteries in the universe than you ever dreamed of!"

As Carruthers thus apostrophised himself, he reached the platform of the railway station just as the train was moving. He made a bold dash for a first-class carriage and scrambled in. On seating himself and looking round, he saw that he was not alone; a lady dressed in black and wearing a thick veil was seated in the further corner opposite him. Carruthers felt a peculiar thrill pass through his nerves as he more closely examined her appearance. "Could it possibly be the Woman in Black? Yes? No? By Heaven, it is!" he exclaimed under his breath. All possibility of doubt was dissipated by the woman addressing him in dulcet tones; at the same time removing her veil and presenting to his astonished gaze features of the most ravishing loveliness.

"Ah! Sir Ashleigh, well met! How more than fortunate you should enter this carriage; and that we should be alone once more! You have,

I hope, been quite well since we last met? You are looking extremely well; indeed, quite yourself."

Carruthers was quite staggered and speechless for a time at the impudence of this address; all he could do at the moment was to scowl darkly. So soon as he could speak, he said:

"I am, as it happens, very well at present, madam; no thanks to you!"

"Sir Ashleigh," she replied, with a look of the most candid innocence on her face, "why do you assume that tone! Surely you are labouring under some delusion. What can have happened to cause a breach of good feeling between us?" At the last words she fixed her lustrous black eyes full upon her companion, with a fixed, concentrated stare until the steady-nerved Carruthers felt his will-power as it were oozing from him by degrees.

Fortunately he knew his danger, and calling forth all his energy to combat the spell of the vampire, he rose to his feet, and exclaimed, in tones as firm as the intensity of his determination could make them:

"Base woman or rather fiend, for there is nothing human in your composition, think not to make me succumb again by your diabolical spells! Your false gods shall no longer protect you! I am now proof against their power! There can be no more intercourse between us. Remember, when we meet, it is war—yes, war to the knife!" Here he showed her a clasp knife, one he had bought to cut a book with. "One step nearer, and not even your sex shall protect you! In killing you I shall be doing humanity a signal service!"

The woman at these terrible words shrunk back into her corner, and a look of fear came over her face.

"Ha!" thought Carruthers, "she dreads physical pain; she is not invulnerable!" Then he remembered a story once told him by his nurse Sarah, to the effect that if you could only draw blood from a witch, she would become as helpless to do evil as an ordinary mortal. This the Woman in Black appeared to know, hence her look of terror. But her wiles were not exhausted, for presently she burst into a peal of rippling, musical laughter most pleasant to the ear. After that she looked Carruthers in the eyes, with an expression of the most bewitching sweetness, which went far towards turning the scale in her favour; and in an enchanting tone of voice, said:

"Oh, Ashleigh, dearest Ashleigh, let me, in heaven's name, try to explain this most painful misunderstanding which now divides us!" As she finished speaking she made a movement towards him.

"Keep off, I say!" Carruthers shouted. "Keep off; or your blood be on your own head!"

"Oh, Ashleigh!" she cried, sinking on her knees before him and raising her hands in supplication, "to think that after all my unbounded love to you—my total surrender to your will—that you, you should long for my death, and be ready to inflict it with your own hand! Where is your heart, Ashleigh, oh, where is your heart?"

Fortunately Carruthers was adamant. He knew the potency of her witching wiles by cruel experience, and had steeled his heart against them by the utmost stretch of his will power. He gazed unmoved at the beautiful, kneeling creature before him, and was even cool enough to observe on one of the raised hands a ring, a plain band of gold without any stone, which was secured against the danger of falling off by a black ribbon fastened to her wrist.

In a moment it flashed on his mind that this was the magic ring; the source of all her horrible power! If he could only gain possession of it, he would rid humanity of a monster more dangerous than plague and pestilence! He fixed his keen, green eye on the ring, and waited his opportunity. The woman continued her pleading with consummate art. She vowed that he was the one man in the world whom she had ever loved; that he, and he alone, was her life and soul; and that if he refused to return her passion, she would die by her own hands! She appealed to his heart, his honour, his sense of manhood, to have a little pity on her, and not callously desert her! While she made this pathetic appeal, real tears streamed down her cheeks, and her voice was nearly choked with sobs. Carruthers, who after all, was made of flesh and blood, and was, indeed, an emotional man, began to feel a lump rising in his throat in spite of himself.

The apparently heartbroken woman, observing this sign of weakness, rose from her knees; and with the spring of a tigress fell upon her victim. But Carruthers was on the alert, and seizing the wrist bound with black ribbon, first severed it, and, then, pulling at one end, the ring fell on the floor of the carriage. To add to the horror of the scene, the train at that moment passed through a long tunnel, and there was no light in the carriage. A desperate struggle took place in the darkness for the possession of the ring. It had apparently rolled under the seat, and neither could find it. Dreading lest it should fall into Carruthers' power, the vampire made a spring at his throat, and in another instant her sharp teeth would have again been embedded in his flesh; but, aware of her murderous purpose, he seized the monster's throat with such a firm grip that, had it been prolonged, must have proved fatal.

At that moment, however, the train emerged from the tunnel, and slowed into the station. A guard came round to look at the tickets. Before giving her own up the Woman in Black, her hair dishevelled and her hat torn and awry, and covered from head to foot with dust, cried out to the man: "I give this man in charge for insulting and assaulting me. Arrest him, at once!"

• • •

CHAPTER XXV

CARRUTHERS WINS AND LOSES THE MAGIC RING

I n spite of the gravity of the charge, which the condition of the woman made more weighty, against a man in the position of Carruthers, he took no notice whatever of it; but while his accuser was making it, occupied himself only in a determined search for the ring, which he was, at last, fortunate enough to find. Having secured it in an inner pocket, he whispered a few words in the ear of the guard, took out one of his visiting cards, and gave it to the man. The guard gave a low whistle as he looked at it. At this moment a police-constable appeared at the carriage door. When Carruthers saw the man, he said: "I charge this woman with wilful murder. She is an escaped prisoner. Confront her with Inspector Jones at Abbotswood; he will confirm my statement. I am Sir Ashleigh Carruthers of Tudor Hall. I shall be ready at any time to give further evidence."

"It is false! It is false! You are a lying villain!" screamed the Woman in Black, in an ecstasy of rage. "You are a common thief, and have stolen my ring!"

"Come, come, my beauty, that won't do!" said the constable. "I happen to know Sir Ashleigh Carruthers by sight, and have heard much about him, so, you see, that tale won't wash. Your appearance corresponds exactly with that in the papers: so just drop that little game, and come quietly along with me!"

Here the officer drew a pair of steel bracelets from his pocket and, with the dexterity which only comes from skill and practice, fixed them on the slender wrists of the Woman in Black.

"What is the meaning of this, constable? How dare you! I tell you I am innocent! I called you in order to give this man into custody. He has insulted me, and stolen my ring. Search him, and you will find my statement is true." This was said by the prisoner in a tone of vehement passion.

Carruthers scribbled the following words on a card, which he handed to the officer: "I have the ring in my pocket. I gained possession of it in order to safeguard society from the attacks of the woman, and am prepared to give my reasons for so doing. Except that charge, nothing she says is true. Inspector Jones, of Abbotswood, will give you all the necessary information."

When the officer had read the writing on the card, he nodded meaningly to Carruthers, as he led his loudly protesting prisoner away. At this moment the train moved slowly out of the station; and the last words Carruthers heard as he watched the officer and prisoner, were hers: "This is scandalous! I tell you it is all a mistake! I protest against this violence! You shall be severely punished for your ruffianly conduct!"

Her passionate protestations were, however, treated with supreme indifference, and the Woman in Black was soon safe under lock and key in a police cell at Slowboro.

Carruthers in a short time was at Tudor Hall, thinking deeply over his exciting adventure, and congratulating himself on its successful issue. After his evening meal, he found it impossible to direct his thoughts in any other direction. "So long," he soliloquized, "as this little ring remains in my possession, the innocent will be free from the murderous attacks of, perhaps, the most inhuman scourge that ever existed; and, better still, it means decay and death to its former possessor!"

Carruthers took the ring out of his pocket and examined it carefully with the help of a powerful lens. That the hieroglyphics were

Egyptian he could see at a glance; also that the engraving was beautiful; but the gold was worn very thin, apparently through centuries of
use. It might, he thought, be strengthened by adding more gold; but
that would diminish its mysterious influence. It would be certain to
wear out in time; and, then the possessor's power would disappear
with it. With these and similar thoughts the evening wore away, and
at midnight Carruthers thought of retiring to rest. But his mind was in
a ferment of agitation; and his nerves vibrated at every little noise and
even at his own movements. At last he resolved to go to his room; and,
after lighting his candle, proceeded to ascend the broad, oaken staircase
leading to it. He felt so nervous, that, every now and then, he stared
at his own shadow; in fact, he never remembered to have had such an
attack of nerves before.

Carruthers' sleeping room was in keeping with the other parts of the
noble hall, which, as its name denotes, was built in the Tudor style of
architecture. The ceiling was low with massive rafters, the walls were pan-
elled and hung with faded tapestry, and over the massive fireplace frowned
a dark portrait of some remote ancestor clad in armour and holding a
marshal's baton. The floor was polished, and on it here and there were
strips of Turkey carpet. The casement was of large and heavy stone;
and the panes of glass small. The furniture was of dark oak; and the
bedstead was an elaborately carved four-poster surrounded by faded
curtains. Carruthers, on entering, placed his candlestick on a massive
oaken chest, and having, as usual, locked his door, he proceeded to
wind up his watch, and, after that, to empty his pockets. Amongst the
miscellaneous things he placed on the chest was the magic ring, which,
he naturally thought, would be perfectly safe there. His intention was
to hand it over to the care of the police the next day. The weather had
been sultry and oppressive, and he opened the window; indeed, it was
his custom to sleep with the window open even in bad weather.

On completing his preparations for rest, he blew out the candle
and jumped into bed. The moon shone so brightly in at the window
that extinguishing the candle made very little difference, except that

the shadows thrown by the stone casement were darker and the silvery moonlight brighter by contrast. Carruthers found it quite impossible to sleep, and as he rested on his elbow, he fixed his eyes on the chest which stood in a corner of the room, which was bright with moonlight. "Great Heavens!" he exclaimed. "What is that! How did those men enter the locked room? They could not enter through the window!" He at first imagined that burglars had made an entrance; but a thought flashed through his mind as he looked at the strange forms and attire of the intruders. There could be no doubt possible about who and what they were. Yes, they were the gods of Egypt, so graphically described by Inspector Jones. There were the hawk-headed deity Horus; Pasht with cat's face; Sebek with the crocodile's hideous head; the bull-headed Apis, and others, including the Hippopotamus-headed Typhon. Amongst these hideous beings was evidently the high priest of Heliopolis in sacerdotal robes, from whose mummy the magic ring had been stolen. These extraordinary beings whispered together and gesticulated occasionally, but no sound of words could be beard by Carruthers. As the wondering man watched them, others entered, till the room seemed full of them. They appeared to come and go without passing through door or window, and the chamber seemed to be transformed into an Egyptian temple.

Carruthers experienced a strange sensation, which was more astonishment than horror, as from a recumbent position he assumed another and sat bolt upright, to enable him to more closely watch the unheard of proceedings. Some of his weird visitors came up to his bed, looked at him, and afterwards glided away. One of them who was near the spot where the ring was deposited, turned to him and pointed the forefinger of his extended right hand, from which a blue phosphorescent flame shot, directly at Carruthers, with the result that he was immediately deprived of all will power and physical strength; and he sat there as if petrified, with his eyes staring into space, unable to utter a word or make a movement. He was completely hypnotised, not in the sense of being sent to sleep; for his mind was as active as ever; he was only deprived of all will power; his own strong volition being subjugated, for the time, by a much more powerful will. "How long will this state of things continue?" he asked himself. Should he ever be able to extricate himself from the control of this powerful god?

As these ideas passed through his brain, a sound of fluttering wings against the window panes caused his heart to stand still, and, the next moment, a huge vampire bat, of a size unknown in this country, entered through the open casement. He felt certain that it was the same bat mentioned more than once in the narrative of the Rev. Jabez Waldegrave, which had proved so nearly fatal both to father and son; in other words it was the astral spirit of the witch that had taken upon itself this degraded form while the earthly body lay asleep in the police cell at Slowboro. Carruthers deemed that his last hour had come. Doubtless the accursed creature, true to the fell instincts of its nature, would fly to him, fasten its fangs upon his throat, and, after drinking the last drop of his life's blood, would fly away, leaving him to die. He knew that he was quite unable to offer any resistance. Oh, that he could muster up sufficient power to enable him to leap from his bed, seize the poker, and dash to pieces the head of the monster before it had time to destroy him! Alas, alas, all his efforts were futile, and he was doomed to watch the movements of the abominable creature as it circled round and round the room with the intention, apparently, of at last settling on him!

The agony of suspense, which, in reality, lasted only for a few minutes, appeared to him an eternity. Suddenly, to his surprise, the creature left him, and made for the corner of the room where the oak chest stood. The gods of Egypt moved aside, and Carruthers clearly saw the foul bat catch up the magic ring with its teeth; and, to his renewed terror, it flew back towards the bed, circled two or three times round his head, struck him a blow in the face with one wing, and then vanished into the night.

It had hardly passed through the window when all the Egyptian gods disappeared in a flash, and Carruthers felt the spell which had held him bound, vanish, and his will and physical vigour return. He jumped out of bed, and his first action was to close the window to prevent the return of the vampire bat. As he did so the proverb about closing a stable door after the horse had bolted recurred to him. "Ah, the accursed brute!" he shouted aloud as he seized the poker and wildly whirled it around his head, and, at last, brought it down on the floor with a loud thud, thus dealing, unfortunately only in imagination, a death blow to the obscene beast he hated. This exhibition of restored physical power appeased him to some extent; he returned to bed and soon sank into a sleep which lasted till late the next morning.

• • •

CHAPTER XXVI
DATED FROM PARIS

When Carruthers awakened, he felt for a time bewildered and uneasy. He had a difficulty in persuading himself that his strange experiences of the past night had not been a dream. Rising in the midst of these reflections, he made for the oak chest to see if the ring had really disappeared. It was not there; it was, indeed, gone! What more proof was requisite to prove that what he had seen was no vision but a fact?

"It passes human experience and all belief," he muttered; "and the worst of all is the fact that by this time the witch has escaped and all my efforts have been thrown away!"

On reaching the breakfast room Carruthers found a letter, with a black edge, on the table, in a familiar handwriting. It was dated from Paris, and Carruthers recognised the hand as that of his old friend, Vincent Cholmondeley. It was as follows:

> Grand Hotel, Paris
> May 5, 1901

My dear old friend, Ashleigh,

I am really at a loss to find words to excuse myself for allowing so long a time to pass without answering your friendly letter; but hope that you will find some extenuation of my fault when you learn the very sad event which had lately thrown a blight over my existence, and caused me to appear neglectful of the best of friends. Alas! how shall I begin? But it must be done, although tears stream from my eyes as I write. Know then, dear old friend, that my beloved wife, to whom I had been so lately united, and who was the life and soul of my existence, whose personal charm and bright mental gifts were the envy of her own sex and evoked the admiration of ours, without whose companionship and winning ways my life must be henceforth a blank, has—think of it, my friend—been prematurely snatched away from me by a cruel death! Can you realise such a thing, my dear Ashleigh, happening in Europe—in a city like Paris—when I tell you that my darling wife, in the very heyday of her youth and beauty, has actually fallen a victim through wounds inflicted on her by the teeth of a vampire bat, presumably escaped from some menagerie, which entered her bedchamber during her sleep? No; you cannot realise anything so apparently impossible and preposterous—in fact, I can hardly believe it myself!

Imagine my feelings, if you can, on waking the following morning and finding myself lying by the side of my dead wife! Oh, the unspeakable horror of it! Such things might have happened in India, where vampires are known to exist; but in civilised Europe— in Paris! It is like an insult to probability and common sense! Do you know, dear Ashleigh, I myself now and again scout the idea, and try to think I have been the victim of a nightmare; that my brain has failed me! What! I am alone in the world; and the body of my dearest and best sleeps in the Protestant cemetery here! In spite of that sad knowledge, I certainly feel her presence. Whenever I am in a pensive mood, thoughts rise in my mind which I know are her thoughts. She also appears to me in dreams and assures me that she is happy and always near me. Indeed, sweet and tender soul, if she were not happy who could ever expect to be so. She bids me not to sorrow for her; that our parting was fated to happen; and that she will wait for me beyond the grave, where all pain and sorrow will forever cease. This is sweet consolation; but to be unable to see her, to hear the tender music of her voice, to miss the gentle touch of her hand, is—well, we

are but mortal, dear friend—is to me, very, very hard to bear! I am
afraid I have said too much concerning my own feelings; and, indeed
were I not certain that my old friend Ashleigh had a kind, generous,
sympathising heart, nothing on earth would have induced me to lay
open my very soul as I have done. But you, dear friend, are not the
man to sneer at the sacredness of grief; to laugh at a man in the deepest trouble, especially when he is your oldest friend; and I, therefore,
feel assured of your heartfelt sympathy for my irreparable loss.

I must conclude this sad letter with ample apologies for its
length, and remain, ever your true, but heart-broken friend,

VINCENT CHOLMONDELEY

P.S. I hope to return home soon, when we can talk over old times
together once more—V.C.

"Good heavens!" exclaimed Carruthers, at the conclusion of the
letter. "Poor dear old Vincent! This is, indeed, a blow! I'll lay my life
his wife's death was the work of the same hellish vampire! Oh, it is
monstrous that this fiend should be allowed to prey on humanity, and
that nothing can be done to destroy her! Poor fellow, I will write to
him at once and express my deep sympathy and sorrow!... I think I
had better, at present, confine my letter to that and say nothing, until
we meet, about my own extraordinary experience."

When he had finished breakfast, Carruthers adjourned to the
library, and wrote his friend a long letter, full of manly sympathy, which
proved that the writer, though a rough soldier, and not possessed of
much eloquence, had a warm and generous heart.

When the letter was finished and ready for the post, Carruthers'
thoughts turned again to his mortal enemy, who, he felt sure, was at
large. He soon made up his mind to visit Slowboro; and on his way see
Nurse Sarah, whom the reader will remember was lodge-keeper at his
friend's place, the Grange. He strolled to the station and took a ticket
for Slowboro. He had not long to wait for a train, and soon reached his
destination, and walked to the police station.

When he was just in front of the place he met, face to face, the constable who had arrested the Woman in Black.

The man, whose name was Matcham, when he recognised Carruthers, looked very confused and distressed.

"Sir Ashleigh," he said, "I have bad news for you."

"I know it," said Carruthers, "that woman has slipped through your fingers."

"How? Have you met her——?" inquired the constable.

"No, I have not; but I knew beforehand that she would escape, and she has done so. Are you surprised? Inspector Jones, of Abbotswood, would not be," said Carruthers.

"Indeed, Sir Ashleigh, I am very much astonished, considering the way she was guarded," replied Matcham.

"I tell you what, my man: stone walls and iron bars cannot hold her. I know that by past experience," replied Carruthers. "Mind, I don't say that any blame attaches itself to you or any other officer. Why, she would slip through the fingers of the devil himself. The woman is a witch and possessed of infernal powers!"

At these strange words, Matcham looked scrutinisingly at Carruthers' face much in the same way that Inspector Jones had done before, and with the same motive. Observing that no smile appeared on Carruthers' face, but, on the contrary, it expressed the utmost earnestness and conviction, Matcham looked down and thoughtfully examined his boots for a few minutes, and then said very slowly:

"If that is the case, Sir Ashleigh—and I am sure you would not joke on such a subject—I say, supposing that is the case, may I ask what your motive was in giving such a person into custody?"

"Wait, my man; I am coming to that. I told you I had obtained her ring by stratagem, didn't I? You heard her accuse me of stealing it; and that was what she wished to give me in charge for?"

"That's all perfectly correct, Sir Ashleigh."

"And I then and there promised to explain the matter. Now, this is the explanation. The ring in question is a magic ring. How she obtained it heaven only knows; but so long as it is in her possession she is endowed with supernatural power which enables her to defy the police, and, indeed, everybody else. She can render herself invisible, burst through stone walls and leave no mark of her exit; in fact, there are few things she cannot do; that is, if the devil permits it.... But without the ring she is helpless and subject to the same laws that govern ordinary humanity. Now, this ring has been lost before, and with disastrous consequences to the woman; but this later. She subsequently regained possession of it, and by its means escaped from the police cell at Abbotswood. I met her by chance yesterday in a railway carriage and observed the magic ring on her finger, secured to her wrist by a black ribbon. Well, to be brief, I cut the ribbon and gained, after a severe struggle, possession of the ring; and, then, as you know, gave her into your charge."

"And yet, Sir Ashleigh, although you had the wonderful ring in your hands, she still managed to escape from us. How was that?"

"Now I am coming to the most wonderful part of my story; and I warn you that the plain facts will severely tax your faith," said Carruthers, and related fully the way in which the magic ring was lost.

To merely say that Matcham was astonished is to very inadequately describe his state of mind. He returned to the station speechless with astonishment.

• • •

CHAPTER XXVII
A BIT OF LACE

T he story that Carruthers told Matcham was made as plain as human language could make it; the narrator went most carefully into every detail; and the result was that the hard-headed, matter-of-fact constable's scepticism was broken down, and he became quite converted to Carruthers' views of the case. But to arrive at a common conclusion as to what should be done towards tracking the witch was a different matter; and neither Carruthers nor he could fix on any practical resolution. It was nearly mid-day when Carruthers left Matcham, who, we must say, was a wiser and sadder man than before the meeting. The former set out briskly for the Grange to call on Nurse Sarah, who happened to see him coming, through the lodge window, and hurried out to the open gate.

"Good morning, Sir Ashleigh, I hope you are well, sir!"

"Yes, nurse, thank you; very well considering."

"Considering; yes, Sir Ashleigh, that's it, considering."

"What do you mean, nurse?" demanded Carruthers.

"Well, Sir Ashleigh, considering that because you would not listen to your old nurses's advice, and have had to suffer in consequence—Oh, I know all about it!"

"All right, nurse, I don't attempt to deny it or disguise anything. I have suffered, and don't dispute the fact. I should have taken your warning to heart! but who would have foreseen such a catastrophe? As a matter of course I set your words down to rank superstition; and who would not have done the same?"

"But now you have grown wiser you will say," said Sarah.

"Well, I hope so," said Carruthers. "We all live and learn; or, rather, ought to do so. By the bye, what news have you had of your master? Have you received the sad intelligence?"

"Yes, Sir Ashleigh, I had a telegram saying as how my poor mistress was dead, and that master was coming home alone soon."

"Nothing further, nurse?" On receiving a negative reply, Carruthers went on to say, "Well, I received a letter from my friend this morning, which gives certain details which I am sure will interest you; and my object in calling was to read you certain parts of the letter."

"Thank you, Sir Ashleigh; but before you do so, perhaps you will take a little snack to eat?"

"Well, nurse, thank you, I will, as it is now past one o'clock, and I have had a fairly good walk." After satisfying his hunger, he had a long talk with Sarah. On his way back to the station he thought over her words, especially of the old couplet:

> *Vervain and dill*
> *Keep witches from their will.*

The old woman had so much faith in the saying, that she insisted on giving him a packet of the two herbs, and made him promise to keep it on his body for protection against witchcraft.

"Who knows," he said to himself, "but what there may be some truth in the ancient adage? There can, however, be no harm in trying it; and as to being considered superstitious, I feel able to believe in almost anything now." He had by this time reached the station, and when his train steamed in he entered an empty carriage. The train was soon in motion, and as he grew tired of looking vacantly at the flat and monotonous scenery which flashed past him, he mechanically directed his attention to the interior of the carriage.

He soon, however, grew interested, as he became convinced that it happened to be the very compartment in which he had recently travelled with the Woman in Black with such dramatic results. He had not noted the number of the carriage, nor was there anything peculiar in the fittings to distinguish it from any other one. What was it, therefore, which enabled him to distinguish it? It was this. As his eyes examined the floor, he noticed that it had been carelessly swept, and enough dust remained to show the impression of a small, delicate hand with taper fingers. This to Carruthers was quite sufficient proof to convince him that the compartment was identical with the one in which he had had his encounter with the witch.

But further confirmation was to hand. On more carefully examining the dust under the seat, Carruthers discovered the impression made by the magic ring itself; and likewise that of his own fingers when he seized it. In addition to this, he found a small portion of a black lace veil which had evidently been torn off in the scuffle. Without knowing why he did so, Carruthers picked it up and placed it carefully in his purse. It was not, he thought, likely to serve any practical purpose; but it would, at least, remind him of his extraordinary encounter with the Woman in Black. On reaching Fuddleton Station, Carruthers noticed a group of his neighbours on the platform talking excitedly together. He very much desired to avoid them, recognising them all as typical specimens of the genus "local gossip", of whom he had a wholesome horror. It was absolutely necessary, however, that he should pass them in order to leave the station. From what he could not help hearing, they seemed to have all just arrived by the London train, and were so absorbed in some interesting topic that they did not notice him as he passed quickly by to give up his ticket. He caught a few words uttered by a plethoric local dignitary.

"I have been credibly informed that the London police are already in pursuit of her, and do not despair of a capture."

"Oh, I do hope the wicked wretch will be caught!" interrupted a woman's shrill voice. "Hanging is too good for her! I wouldn't like to be Sir Ashleigh Carruthers to be mixed up with such an affair, and he so reserved, too! *He! he! he!*"

Carruthers waited for no more, but walked briskly home, and, on arriving there, went at once to the library, threw himself into an easy chair, and was soon lost in thought.

"What can these cackling idiots know of the movements of the police? It would be deucedly annoying if I should be called on to give evidence. The worst of it is that, even if I did so, no good could accrue. What can the police—or, indeed, anyone else—do while the fiend remains in possession of the ring? Aye, there's the rub; if she can be deprived of that, we may laugh at her impotence to do harm!"

Carruthers, with all his thinking, could arrive at no feasible idea of how to do the one thing needful; but his determination was fixed never to lose sight of his object, and to do every possible thing to accomplish his purpose.

His thoughts then turned in the direction of Nurse Everest. "How interested she will be," he thought, "in all these occurrences! I will write to her at once." He sat at his writing table and began a long letter containing a most elaborate account of the events that had happened to him since she had returned to London. He posted the letter himself, when finished, and returned in time for dinner. For some reason Carruthers felt that he had done the right thing in sending the letter. He could not account for it; but he felt more at ease. He did not really think that she could do anything for him; but he had promised to keep her informed of everything relating to the Woman in Black; and, perhaps, his satisfaction arose from having kept his word. It was with much surprise that he received an answer to his letter two days later. It was couched in modest and respectful terms, well spelt, well written, and, in short, evidently the letter of a lady. Nurse Everest first thanked Carruthers for his long and interesting epistle, which she had read with great pleasure, adding that he overrated her humble services, but trusted that in the future she might be the means of assisting him in another way, *viz.*, in helping him to bring the arch-criminal to justice. To Carruthers' surprise she attached great importance to the fragment of black lace, to which, in truth, he had hardly given a thought, found in the railway carriage, and begged him to send it to her by return of post, without allowing anyone to see or to handle it but himself.

"I wonder," muttered Carruthers, "what the little woman can want it for? What does she imagine she can do? Some caprice, I suppose. Well, well, it can do no harm to gratify her." He immediately enclosed the bit of lace in an envelope addressed to Nurse Everest, added a few kindly words, and despatched the letter.

Although Carruthers spent the rest of the day looking after the workmen, and in other ways attending to his affairs, the one absorbing topic which occupied all but the surface of his mind was the Woman in Black; how to capture her and safeguard the innocent from the attacks of such a terrible scourge.

• • •

CHAPTER XXVIII
A MYSTERIOUS POWER

N urse Everest had never confided to Carruthers, during the
time she had attended to him, that she was the possessor
of a very extraordinary gift, that of psychometry. Very few
persons outside the inner circle of occultism have even ever heard
the word. For this reason an explanation of its meaning is due to the
reader. Such terms as clairvoyance, mesmerism, hypnotism, thought
reading, palmistry, spiritualism, and crystal gazing, are, of course,
known to all. Second sight, which some believe to be a special gift of
the Scotch, is also known to most people.

But psychometry, another gift of the spirit, which, in company
with the foregoing, bigots of all denominations, both religious and
scientific, have agreed to howl down, if possible, is much less known,
at least, by its name. To explain the term then: psychometry is a gift,
latent, perhaps, in all; but only found in its highest development in a
chosen few, by means of which the adept is enabled by a certain subtlety
of touch to call up in vision before his mind's eye all the circumstances
and surroundings of the person or object subject to his examination,
through something that that person has worn on the body, or been in
close personal contact with.

Professor Reichenbach, in treating "radiant matter," discovered
that every object, whether animate or inanimate, possesses a subtle
fluid or aura of its own surrounding it, resembling the halo or nimbus
round the heads of saints in Roman Catholic pictures. It is this subtle

aura which is detected by the fine perception of the adept, and enables him or her when handling a piece of inert matter to determine what hands it has passed through, whether it has crossed the water and visited other countries; or, that makes the seer capable of describing the outward appearance as well as the inward character of those persons who have had it in their possession, or with whom it has come in contact.

These facts in modern science, unwelcome alike to religious bigots and pseudo scientists, are nevertheless grounded on a scientific basis of fact which renders them impregnable, let fanatics protest as they may. "*Magna est veritas et prevalebit.*" Here is an illustration of our theory. Let us suppose that a small piece of stone, say from an Egyptian pyramid, be given into the hands of a psychometer—male or female. Children under the age of twelve, young unmarried girls, or persons of essentially pure lives for preference, as being the most untroubled and lucid in mind. Without giving the adept any clue whatever to the origin of the stone, he or she will see in vision the surroundings of it from the moment it was picked up at the base of the pyramid, and be able to describe the people, their nationality, and costume, who happened to be present at the time. More wonderful still, the adept will be able to see far back into the past, and be able to describe the workmen employed in building that pyramid, and even behold them fitting an enormous stone into its destined place, of which the piece in his hands is only a fragment. The adept will describe the climate, the various costumes of the people who have visited the spot from age to age, until he sees, at last, the identical stone being cut out of the solid rock, and transported by huge engines and great physical labour to the spot where it was required.

The sceptic will, perhaps, ask how we are to know whether the so-called adept is speaking the truth and faithfully describing what he professes to see, or is only drawing on his imagination and trying to deceive? In answer to this objection, we advise that every possible precaution should be taken to prevent imposture. The adept should have no clue whatever as to where the object handed to him comes from. The same object might be given to another adept unknown to the first one, so as to render collusion impossible, and their descriptions compared. The probity also of the adept should be above suspicion.

* * * * *

We will now return to Nurse Everett, who was alone in her room, and had just opened Carruthers' letter which contained the piece of lace found by him in the railway carriage after his encounter with the Woman in Black. As the young girl seized it eagerly, yet loathingly, a shudder which shook her from head to foot passed through her frame. "Horrible! Oh, horrible!" she whispered, "I see blood everywhere— yes—and there is that fiend of a woman again just as she appeared in my dream, dressed in black and with blood oozing from the corners of her mouth! . . . I can look no more. I cannot bear it! . . . Ah! she is there again; but no longer young and handsome. See; she has shrivelled into an aged and decrepit crone! What is she doing now? Oh, the wretch!" She has caught up a healthy living child; she has her teeth in its throat, and is draining its life's blood! Now a hand is placed on her shoulder. She is in the custody of the police. They have locked her up for the night in a cell. . . . How is this? She is no longer in prison. She is at large; and once more young and beautiful! Oh, how I loathe her! . . . See, see! she is now in a railway carriage alone—No, not alone! There is a man there; and I know him! Yes, it is Sir Ashleigh Carruthers. Heaven guard him! What! They are quarrelling! The ring drops from her hand—the ring; the magic ring! They are passing through a tunnel, and both are on the floor of the carriage scrambling for the ring! Now the train stops at a station. I see it all! Now she is in the hands of the police, and the train moves on with Sir Ashleigh in it. How wonderful! It is all just as he described it in his letter. Now I see water. She is on board a steamer. She has left the country. All the scenes she has travelled through pass rapidly before my eyes. I seem to be in a warmer climate; the air is balmy;

the sea and landscapes are steeped in brilliant sunshine. There are beautiful buildings, lovely gardens filled with exquisite flowers; and the sea, how blue it is! The place is filled with fashionable people of different nationalities, though many of them are dark like Italians. There are also many English and Americans walking on the terraces overlooking the sea. Now I see a lady exquisitely dressed and remarkably beautiful. She is surrounded by gentlemen, who follow and pay her the most marked attention. What! can it be? Yes, yes; it is—the Woman in Black; but now she is dressed in the most exquisitely harmonised colours. She lives here in grand style; has luxurious apartments, and is always surrounded by the best company in the place. She is now entering a beautiful building. What place is it? Why, it must be a palace devoted to gambling! There is a long table and people sitting, and others standing or playing, or waiting to do so. When the witch enters the people make way for her. See, she stakes gold and wins, then she repeats her play and wins again and again. She always wins."

At this point Nurse Everest broke off as if exhausted. "I can see no more today," she said. "I must not exert myself too much, for I am feeling very unwell." She sat down and fell into a deep sleep, which lasted two hours. She rose refreshed, but would not look at or touch the black lace again during the day. She was not so strong as she had been, and had, indeed, been advised to try a change of air. It was her intention to start the next day for a holiday of three weeks. Before going she wrote a long letter to Carruthers, thanking him for sending the piece of lace, and describing to him in full the visions that had appeared to her through its means. She told him of her intention of going away for a time, and promised to write should anything occur throwing light on the mystery they both so intensely desired to solve. She posted the letter herself, packed her trunk, and left the nurses' home for her vacation.

• • •

CHAPTER XXIX
A SUICIDE AT MONTE CARLO

◯

"Strange! Very strange!" muttered Carruthers the next morning, as he toyed with Nurse Everest's letter. "That certain privileged persons should possess such abnormal gifts! What does it depend on? It certainly cannot be acquired. I should not think of doubting her veracity for a moment; she is as truthful as she looks. Yet, after all, what does it lead to? The only point to be considered is this: Will it assist in bringing that fiend to a long delayed punishment? Will it deprive her of the possession of the magic ring? I greatly doubt it. . . . So the little woman is enjoying her holiday now, and she well deserves it. She is a sweet, pure-hearted girl, just the type I admire; it is a pity it is so rare. A loving, self-sacrificing woman who finds happiness in devoting herself to others without a thought of gain! Ah! what an example she sets to the empty-headed, frivolous, fashionable portion of her sex, whose only ambition is to outdo each other in the extravagance of dress, the silliness of their talk and their power to attract idiots of the opposite sex for the sole purpose of arousing the envy of their so-called friends" Such persons are really destitute of all that constitutes a real woman: brains, heart, and conscience!"

After this fierce and ungrateful attack on the sex which had surrounded him with so much flattery and attention, Carruthers fell into a reverie; and soon after, loading his favourite pipe with the tobacco he preferred, began thinking of how to capture the Woman in Black.

Even this topic tired him in time; and he took up a newspaper and carelessly perused it, until his eye fell on a paragraph which held his attention. It was as follows:

An inquest was held last Tuesday, at the ———Hotel, Monte Carlo, on the body of Lieutenant Adolf von Rosenberg, of H.I.H. Hussars, who was discovered covered with blood in the part of the cemetery used for suicides, just outside the gambling saloon.

The deceased was well known to have been an inveterate gambler for years, and is reported to have been generally unlucky at play, his family having frequently paid his debts of honour. He had recently visited his father at Munich, and being then deeply involved, implored him to rescue him from disgrace for the last time. His father, after reproving him severely for his past reckless conduct, finished by giving him a large sum of money, with the solemn injunction to pay with it all his debts, and never to trouble him again. The young officer promised earnestly to do this; but the spirit of the infatuated gambler was too strong for him, and, instead of fulfilling his promise, he returned at once to Monte Carlo, staked in a few hours the whole sum, and lost. Anguish and despair gripped him; and, rushing to the part of the cemetery where suicides are buried, he put an end to his worthless existence. The deceased is reported to have been deeply enamoured of a fashionable Russian lady of high rank, whose rare personal charms and great mental gifts have attracted round her a host of admirers of the sterner sex. It is said that Lieutenant von Rosenberg did not despair of winning her for himself, and thought that only his poverty stood in his way. He imagined that if he could only amass at the gaming table a large fortune, all obstacles would be removed.

At the report of the pistol, several *habitués* rushed out and ran to the spot, but found that they were not the first on the scene. A lady, closely veiled, was bending over the body, apparently kissing its dead lips. She hurried away at the approach of strangers, and, by the bright light of the moon, it was observed that her rich dress was much stained with blood.

"Humph!" muttered Carruthers, when he had read thus far. "I wonder if this story is destined to throw light on—on——? Why, good heavens! It must be the same woman! Yes, it's that accursed vampire, I'll stake my life! What did Nurse Everest say in her letter? The warm climate, the lovely terrace, the flowers, the fashionably dressed people, the gambling palace, the beautiful woman exquisitely dressed! Yes, depend upon it, we have a clue at last! There could not be two such monsters in existence at one and the same time! I wonder whether Nurse Everest has read this account? Most likely not. I will cut it out and send it to her London address, marked to be forwarded. . . . Of course, I may be mistaken; but no chance must be lost in pursuing the fiend!"

Carruthers rose to his feet, and excitedly paced the room for some time; after doing this he walked to the stables, saddled his horse, and galloped over the hills to clear his brain. His favourite horse, which had been his faithful companion during the South African campaign, did not get an outing every day, he was consequently fresh; and feeling the elastic green turf under his hoofs, he bounded away with exuberant spirit. Carruthers wanted a good spin and the horse knew it, and carried him over hedges, ditches, and five-barred gates, till, on nearly reaching home, he was snorting, and appeared greatly blown. Carruthers patted the animal on the neck affectionately, and thus apostrophised him: "This is better than railway travelling, eh, Rover? Better than being strapped up and shipped backwards on a transport like a bale of goods. It is long since we have had such a run as this together; not since we were in action on the wild veldt, I declare!"

The noble animal whinnied by way of expressing his feelings, and appeared to understand every word his master said. Then Carruthers walked his horse gently to the stable, consigned him to the care of a groom, and entered the hall. On the table he found a telegram, and, on opening it, read the following:

"Have altered my mind. Am going south for a change. Will write.—Cholmondeley."

This was disappointing. He had waited day after day for his friend's arrival, and now he was baulked of the friendly talk he had anticipated.

• • •

CHAPTER XXX
ANOTHER VICTIM

More than a fortnight passed away before Carruthers heard from his friend, Vincent Cholmondeley, again. One morning, however, the following letter reached him:

Monte Carlo
June 21, 1901

My dear friend Ashleigh,

What must you think of me for keeping you so long in suspense as to my movements? Private business, and, perhaps, a fit of laziness must plead my excuse. In truth, dear friend, I sadly needed a change. The melancholy and *ennui* consequent on my bereavement have been more than I could bear, and had begun to prey upon my health, so my doctor ordered me a thorough change of scene, and, if possible, cheerful society. Acting on his advice, I packed my portmanteau and prepared to travel south, without any definite purpose. Chance, destiny, or whatever you prefer to term it, landed me in this enchanting place, to which I feel attracted in a manner I never remember to have felt before for any other in the whole course of my travels. Imagine your old friend, if you can, under a clear, cloudless sky, breathing the balmiest air, redolent with the odour of flowers, with the calm Mediterranean, of a deep, sapphire blue, breaking in tiny wavelets at his feet, while behind him stretch hills overgrown with olive trees; and, here and there are the solitary stone pine or cypress, the aloe and the cactus. Then the vine with its luxuriant bunches of ripe, luscious grapes growing at the road-side and inviting the thirsty traveller to pluck and eat. Added to this, I am living in a palace of an hotel, overlooking the sea, and have also made several cheerful acquaintances.

The attraction of the gambling saloon I have not yet men-tioned; but although it comes last, it certainly is not counted least, by the majority here, in the attractions of this delightful place. It is interesting to watch the variety of expressions on the countenances of the votaries of the *"rouge et noir."* The eager expectancy of the timid man as he stakes his two napoleons, perhaps all he has in the world; the triumph which illuminates his face if he wins; the despair which darkens it if he loses; contrasted with the stolid indifference of the "croupier" as he calls out, from time to time, *"Faites vos jeux, messieurs et mesdames,"* and rakes in or pays out what is lost or won, are sights which do not soon tire the thoughtful and interested observer.

You will hardly believe, Ashleigh, but I, even I, have been bit-ten by the prevailing gambling epidemic. This will astonish you after the way you have heard me preach against the system; but, I assure you the spirit of play is in the very air one breathes here. Why, were you here yourself, I should be more than astonished if you did not feel yourself drawn in like all the rest. I was drawn into it by grief and despair, for I found in gambling just the kind of excitement that my mind required to prevent it preying on itself. It drowned the terrible past, and lulled too painful memories to sleep by a species of intoxication. Of course, I know there is another side to the picture. Only a few yards from the superb saloon devoted to play is a ceme-tery reserved for the burial of those unfortunates who end their lives by suicide. You will doubtless have seen in the papers an account of the tragic death of a young German officer after he had ruined himself at the gaming table. There was a romantic love affair mixed up with it, I understand, about which the curious public knew little.

And this brings me to a prominent personage living here, a certain Russian princess of an unpronounceable name. who has succeeded in turning the heads of hundreds of the male sex. She is young and marvellously beautiful, with glorious black eyes and hair, and exquisitely graceful carriage; and lives here in a villa of her own in grand style, charming everyone by her fascinating manners and brilliantly witty conversation. Like all Russians, she is a good linguist, and able to talk with all her admirers in their own tongue. Her parents must have spent a fortune on her education, for I can assure you there is not a subject anyone can mention that she is not able to throw light upon. It has been my good fortune to be introduced to this charming lady, and I can say for myself that her knowledge of English is perfect. There is not even the slightest trace of foreign accent; and I can say the same of other languages in which I have heard her converse.

I am able to add, I think, without conceit, that I am on almost intimate terms with this paragon of talent and beauty, who treats me very graciously whenever we meet. She professes great admiration for the English people, averring that her great delight would be to live in England. This, perhaps, seems strange to you coming from a Russian; does it not? In addition to her supereminent personal charms and real intellectual gifts, she has given evidence of possessing a good heart; and, on many occasions, when my funds have been low, and I have been embarrassed by my losses at the gaming table, this angel of light has lent me sums to go on with out of pure sympathy with my weakness. The way in which she herself wins is marvellous. I really don't think that anybody has ever known her to lose. The source of her enormous wealth is a mystery. She must possess mines of gold to enable her to throw away the yellow metal as she does.

"Humph" muttered Carruthers, "this continual luck at play looks like witchcraft. Then, in addition, her marvellous beauty and fascination, her supreme intellectual gifts! Why, there can be little doubt, especially after Nurse Everest's letter, that it is the same woman! Yes, the plot thickens. We are getting on her track at last!

I must write to warn Vincent before it is too late, or he will be making a fool of himself; in fact, I fear, from the tone of his letter, that he has already done so. There is not a moment to be lost. Why, his life is in absolute danger!"

Without a moment's delay Carruthers sat at his writing table and penned the following epistle to his friend:

My dear friend Vincent,

I am grieved to be obliged to tell you that your letter has impressed me with the direst forebodings. That the fascination of the gaming table may allure a man in your condition of mind and heart is intelligible, however much to be deplored, but, unfortunately, there are other fascinations more deadly still, which wreck both body and soul, and which I, as your oldest friend, would save you from. Don't trust yourself, but fly at once! Come back to England, and we will travel together—anywhere you like, but do not stay where you now are! If you are wise, you will take my advice before you are utterly and for ever buried in a quagmire of moral filth! I know well that such advice is not palatable, but at the risk of wounding your feelings I warn you, in the name of our long friendship, that you are standing on the edge of a bottomless abyss!

Believe me this is no ordinary caution; it is like that a father might give to an only son, warning him not to marry a woman who would bring dishonour on his name. Your case is infinitely more dangerous. I tell you distinctly and solemnly, Vincent, that your very life is in danger! Do not think that I exaggerate or that I am under some strange delusion! I think I know your Russian princess with the unpronounceable name; by the way, she is no more Russian than you are; in fact, I may have been more intimate with her than you imagine, and could tell you many a strange story about her from personal experience, and much more by well-tested report. But in case you may think that I had been led away by mere idle gossip, I can personally vouch for the fact that she is much "wanted" by the police, and, by heavens I'll do all I can to assist them in their efforts to capture her!

She is well known in the neighbourhood in which I now write, and is commonly spoken of as the Woman in Black; or, the Black Lady by the poor people, by whom she is looked upon with dread; and, let me add, for very good reasons. Why, man alive, have you any idea of what that "angel of light" is who seems to have engrossed your whole being? Of course you have not; and, therefore, I will inform you that she is a murderess of the most malignant type, a lying adventuress and impostor, and, as if that were not enough, I will add that she is not even human! Start not, my friend, at so bold an assertion, when I tell you that the idol of your heart, the angel of light, is a living vampire. And that her only hold upon human life is maintained by sucking the blood from living creatures! I fancy I see a sceptical smile steal over your countenance as you read these lines, and almost hear the sigh that escapes you as you think pityingly of my deplorable, mental decline. Alas! my dear Vincent, it is not, as you fondly suppose, that your old friend's wits have given way through sickness or some severe mental strain. I know too well the absolute truth of what I am now writing, because I myself have been brought to the brink of the grave through her diabolical influence, as have many others. Do you still doubt me? Well you shall be placed in a position which will enable you to test my statements, for if the goddess should indeed be the fiendish creature I assert her to be, and it is incredible that two such beings should be in existence at the same time, I will give you the means of knowing that what I assert is God's truth, and not a lie. In the first place, then, the partial description you have given me of your paragon of women agrees in every particular with the monster that exists in my mind's eye; but I will finish the portrait that you have begun.

She is rather tall, her hair and eyes are black, her eyebrows darkly pencilled, her complexion so pallid that it might fairly be termed deathly, while her lips, which are full and beautifully formed, might strike anyone, at first sight, as too brightly red to be natural. Her teeth are pearly white, while her eye teeth are rather too pronounced to be quite in accord with strict beauty; but to all this there is one drawback, her breath is rank and makes one think of the odour of a graveyard. Is that description correct? Does it complete the portrait of the "angel of light"? But I have not yet finished, and will proceed. Examine her ears, and if you do not find that they are pointed at the top like those of some wild animal, never more place faith in your old friend, Ashleigh! Her fingers, too, are claw-like, after the manner of birds of prey. Her eyes are large, soft, and languishing, and remarkably intelligent in expression. Her movements and gestures are graceful and queen-like; her features classical and capable of every variety of expression. One thing more, the most important point of all! She wears on a finger of her left hand, doubtless with many other apparently more valuable rings, a plain band of gold, much worn by time, engraved on the inside with Egyptian hieroglyphics. This is a magic ring which she prizes more than all the world possesses, for by its aid she is enabled to accomplish all her sorceries; without it she is powerless. If you could once possess yourself of this—but there, it is impossible to write all I wish to say in a letter, but I have said enough to warn you. Your fate, your life or death, is in your own power! Heed my warning and live; neglect it and die! Now, my dear Vincent, confess that I have given you a full and graphic description of your idol. I must now say adieu, or I shall be too late for the post, and time is now a question of life and death!

Your sincere friend,

ASHLEIGH CARRUTHERS

After addressing this letter, Carruthers posted it himself.

• • •

CHAPTER XXXI

THE FOOL
AND THE VAMPIRE

◯

As Vincent Cholmondeley was crossing the threshold of his hotel at Monte Carlo one glorious morning late in July, the head waiter hurried after him, and placing a letter in his hand, was in the act of retiring, when the former called out, "Stay! How long has this letter been here? Why, I see by the postmark that it was posted a month ago!"

"Sir, I know nothing; it is the first time I have set eyes on it," answered the man. "Sometimes letters do get delayed for some reason or other."

"It is scandalous! I'll write to *The Times* about it; and expose the negligence of the postal authorities here."

The waiter shrugged his shoulders and disappeared.

A glance at the handwriting sufficed to inform Vincent Cholmondeley that the letter was from Ashleigh Carruthers. He tore open the envelope and extracted the epistle, and, in another moment, he would have read it, when, raising his eyes through some unconscious influence, he beheld gliding gracefully toward him, the exquisite form of the woman he already idolised, clad in the lightest and most delicate summer attire, who, as the reader already knows, was the creature already so often termed in these pages, the Woman in Black; but whom Cholmondeley believed to be a Russian Princess, and, in addition, "an angel of light."

His beloved wife, so recently buried in the Protestant cemetery at Paris, for whom he had expressed such undying love and devotion, was now, alas! for human frailty, completely forgotten, and he had succumbed to the fatal seductions of a siren; had proposed for her hand, and been accepted.

Preparations for the approaching marriage had been discussed between them; there had been no difference of opinion, and Cholmondeley believed himself to be the happiest man alive. At sight of this, to him, heavenly vision, all other thoughts were blotted out, and carelessly thrusting his friend's letter in his outer breast pocket, he hurried to meet his enchantress, with beaming eyes, and outstretched hands: "What! so early abroad, my angel! I was dreaming of you all last night."

"Were you, dearest," she said, in tones of the most seductive sweetness, and with looks that might excuse a stronger willed man than Vincent Cholmondeley for being conquered. "And so was I of you! Ah, how delicious it is when two manifestly twin souls like ours meet on the earth, who are destined to be united both there and in eternity, heedless of the restraints, prejudices, and limitations of this mundane sphere that so degrade beings of grosser clay! We, strong in each other's love, stand hand in hand, and form a force capable of defying the attacks of enemies who are ever on the alert to drag down to their own base level, souls of nobler and loftier strain!"

"My angel!" exclaimed the ecstatic Vincent, as he gazed in rapture into the luminous depths of the dark eyes which looked love at him.

"And you really do love me, my Vincent, really and truly?"

"Love thee, my princess! Have I ever truly loved anyone but thee?"

"And your late wife?" inquired the enchantress.

"Name her not!" affirmed her lover; "I did not know what love was at that time. She was young, pretty, amiable, and affectionate; and, indeed, all that most men would desire; one to toy with in the heart's lighter moments; but she could not feed and fill my soul as thou dost—ah, no, no! We were not born for each other. . . . She has gone, poor child; let her soul rest in peace!"

* * * * *

One might without much stretch of the imagination hear the demons of the nethermost depths of hell laugh *ho! ho! ho! ha! ha! ha!* at this monstrous speech of the bewitched man.

"We have heard something like this before, eh, brother Lucifer?" said Belphegor, when his laughter was exhausted, as he dug his demon brother in the ribs with his elbow.

"Yes, yes, often, very often! *Ha! ha! ho! ho!*"

* * * * *

"And this great passion of yours is only of a month's growth! Will it last, think you?" inquired his fair tormentor.

"Last! Queen of my heart!" exclaimed the infatuated man. "Aye, as long as the world lasts! As fresh throughout eternity as it is today. I tell thee, Princess, that my love for thee is the one passion of my life. I never did, I never could have loved till now. Thou, and thou alone art my love, my life, my whole existence, and that to all eternity!"

* * * * *

At this the merry devils down below roared till they nearly cracked their iron ribs.

* * * * *

The lovers glided on side by side, beguiling the time with amorous talk, when Vincent observed the Princess turn her head as if scanning a group of figures in the distance.

"You are rather absent-minded, Princess, this morning," said Vincent, who, with all the natural egotism of a lover, resented all appearance of interest in anything or anybody but himself.

"Am I, darling? I was only looking at the group of people over there. I do believe there is that wretched little hospital nurse wheeling that bloated-looking, paralytic man in a bath-chair again. She who won over a hundred napoleons off me at roulette yesterday. Do you remember?" The look on the lady's face was of the most venomous kind, and the tone of her voice was such that had not Vincent been a love-sick fool, he would have noticed both; and perhaps, been saved.

"Yes, I remember, Princess. I observed her closely, and thought she was rather pretty."

"Pretty! Well, there is no accounting for taste," replied the lady bitterly.

"Of course, her ordinary style of prettiness could not compare with the sublime beauty of my own Princess!" added Vincent apologetically.

"Oh" pray don't think that I am in the least jealous!" observed the lady.

"No, indeed, that would be too silly; but what is it that you appear to dislike in her?" Vincent asked, a little disturbed by this display of spite in an angel of light.

"She is repugnant to me. I can't say more," she replied.

"Indeed! And why? Is it because she won your money at the gaming table?" inquired the tactless Vincent, who little thought he was playing with fire.

"Boy!" flashed the lady, "you ought to know by this time that I care no more for money than I do for the dust under my feet!"

"That has always been my firm conviction," Vincent replied. "Then, may I ask, on what is your repugnance founded?" he asked.

"Well, I will satisfy you! Whenever I play, whether for large stakes or small, I am always accustomed to win. I cannot help doing so. I was born so; some people are. I never remember to have lost at all; and yet, when that woman appeared on the scene, my luck deserted me."

"You cannot begrudge her her little gains?" said Vincent, who was beginning to open his eyes.

"Fool!" cried the woman, stamping her foot, and speaking passionately. "Do you think I care for the dross, or who gathers it? I who could throw away thousands—nay, millions, if I choose!"

"Indeed, Princess, I quite believe you! Why, then——"

"Listen!" she said, interrupting him. "To every creature living under the sun is given the power to discover its natural foe. By an unerring instinct the mouse and the bird are informed that the cat and the owl are their enemies. It requires no teaching or experience to warn the fowl from the fox, or the rabbit from the ferret, while nearly all animals and birds stand in dread of their enemy the snake. Man alone, proud of his superior origin, which makes him draw a strong line of demarcation between himself and the animal world, refuses to claim any faculty that he fears would place him in the same category as the brute creation, and proudly vaunts his own human reason. As a punishment for his presumption in rejecting everything that his limited human intellect fails to explain, the natural instincts with which Nature has endowed him in common with the brutes, have become blunted through disuse. He is ashamed to harbour a presentiment or forewarning of evil, because, forsooth, the world—his world—would call him superstitious! What a contemptible creature man is after all! To our sex, however, which is less arrogant than yours, in that we make no pretence to explain every mystery by human reason; to our sex indeed has been given a delicacy of perception, a fineness of intuition which to you male animals must often appear miraculous and incredible. Some of us are, of course, more highly gifted than others; and these have also strengthened their instincts by obedience and careful cultivation. When humanity has in the future risen to a higher plane, it will gratefully acknowledge the gifts of instinct and intuition and profit by them.

"It will not only possess every grade and kind of instinct common to the lower kingdoms of animal life; but all those gifts will be greatly intensified."

While this lengthy speech was being delivered, with the greatest animation, Vincent Cholmondeley gazed at the beautiful speaker with the utmost astonishment and admiration.

After a rather lengthened pause, he inquired deferentially:

"Am I then to understand that you, dear Princess, consider yourself to be one of those advanced beings, those pioneers of a new humanity, who are destined to revolutionise our planet?"

"You may do so, if you desire. I am descended from an exceedingly ancient race, whose origin extends far back into the misty past; and of whom only a very few are left. We have preserved the old traditions of our distant ancestors. Our lives and habits are different from those of the mortals of today."

"I thought you were a Russian," said the bewildered Vincent.

"Bah! What matters it what I am! I have lived in Russia, and that has made me familiar with the language; just as I have mastered many other European tongues; and likewise those of Asia. Each of the many countries I have lived in might claim me for a native, so thoroughly at home do I feel in them all."

"What a wonderful woman you are!" exclaimed the fascinated listener.

"It suits my convenience to adopt a country for a time in order to silence the foolish wonder of busy-bodies. People will insist on knowing everything about me, and as I cannot explain everything to their dull intellects, I invent a tale for them adapted to their small capacity of understanding."

Instead of this callous, and obviously unprincipled statement producing its proper effect in her listener, he broke forth with the following burst of admiration:

"Oh, you marvellous being! From the first I perceived that you were one of a different order to all whom I had ever encountered before! Your supernatural beauty, your surprising knowledge of ancient and modern languages and history, which might well excite the surprise and envy of experts; and, in addition, your marvellous intelligence, and all this comprised in one so young as yourself, staggers belief."

"So young! Ha! ha! ha!" interrupted the lady, laughing heartily and ironically.

Even the mocking and ironical laugh pleased the doomed Vincent; and the two lovers sauntered on slowly, side by side, until they reached the base of an olive-clad hill, and here, on its verdant, flower-decked slope, they sank down to rest.

• • •

CHAPTER XXXII
THE CALF SLAUGHTERED

T he sun shone with almost intolerable heat, the mosquitoes were getting too troublesome, and Vincent before seating himself by the side of his beloved, took out his pocket handkerchief to wipe his brow and to drive away the flies. In doing this the letter from Ashleigh Carruthers fell from his pocket into the lap of the *soi-disant* Russian Princess, without his observing it. The lady's eyes were, however, sharper, and noticing that her lover was oblivious of the loss, she hastily glanced at the superscription, and, then, thrust the letter into her pocket without a word.

"Why do you look so pale, my beloved? You are positively ghastly!" said the alarmed lover.

"Am I dearest?" she replied in languid tones. "The heat is so oppressive, but it will soon pass off."

"Take a drop out of my flask," suggested Vincent in alarm.

"No, thank you, Vincent. I am better now," she replied, waving the flask away with her hand. "That is poison to me. See, I am quite well again."

Observing that the normal colour, which was the slightest imaginable, had returned to her cheeks, Vincent's fears abated, and he sank again at her feet.

Presently she said in a voice scarcely audible, "I feel so sleepy, darling, and should enjoy a doze very much, so I am going to cover my face to protect it from the mosquitoes, and I advise you to do the same. Pray don't disturb me; I wish to be perfectly quiet."

"You are quite right, dearest; it will do you good and restore your nerves," answered Vincent, who then proceeded to cover his own face with his red silk handkerchief, and the two were soon lying near each other perfectly still. In a few minutes Vincent Cholmondeley was in a sound sleep, and we are sorry to admit, snoring loudly.

This was what the Russian Princess, the angel of light and vampire, had been patiently or impatiently waiting for. She raised herself from her recumbent position, and leaning on her elbow, looked intently at her victim, and fully satisfying herself that he was in a profound sleep, she took the stolen letter from her pocket, and read it from beginning to end. The reason she had turned so ghastly pale when she first glanced at the letter was because she had seen the signature of Carruthers on the part of the epistle which protruded from the open envelope. So Vincent knew Carruthers! Her keen intuition at once scented danger. If harm could reach her it would be from her most determined enemy. What did the two men, Vincent and Carruthers, know of each other? She must find out. She sat thinking for some time after reading the denunciation of herself; then said, half aloud:

"Well, it is lucky that this letter has fallen into my hands before he had had time to read it. My Egyptian gods still serve me well, I see! I must put an end to this correspondence; and that I'll soon do." Here she crumpled the letter in her hand, and thrust it into her pocket, preparatory to destroying it altogether. She continued ruminating over the contents of the epistle; and presently muttered: "What was it he said in it about me, the insolent villain? My breath was foul! Faugh! oh, it is scandalous! But I do not fear him; I am too well protected. Does he dare to pit himself against me? I have outwitted him before, and will do so again. Aye, everyone who dares to stand before me and bar my way shall die—die—die!" And in the intensity of her passion, she raised her voice in a *crescendo* scale, "like this shallow fool," looking with contempt at the sentimental idiot at her feet. "Yes, he is easily disposed of." As she uttered these words, Vincent stirred and made a movement as if about to rise, taking the red handkerchief in his hand, and at the same time gazing at the woman. "Had he overheard her?" she wondered. "Was there a faint gleam of surprise and suspicion in his eyes; or was it only her fancy?"

But at this moment her attention was attracted by something which appeared on the top of the hill-side, clearly outlined against the sky-line. It was an overdriven bull which was snorting, bellowing, and furiously pawing the earth with its hoofs, at only a short distance from herself and Vincent. The bull saw the red handkerchief and made furiously for them. The danger was imminent, and the woman shrieked out in wild alarm. "Vincent, quick, save me, save me, my Vincent, if you love me!"

Vincent was on his feet in a moment and, gallantly throwing himself between the animal and the woman, seized its horns. He had not the presence of mind to throw away the red rag, which dangled from one hand right in the eyes of the savage brute, increasing its rage tenfold. A terrific struggle began between man and animal, which ended by the latter throwing Vincent high into the air, from which he descended, falling with a heavy thud on the earth, where he lay stunned and helpless. Turning to the prostrate body of his foe, the brute sniffed at him; and, then, as if inspired by a happy thought, prodded him with his horns, goring him severely, and proceeded to do so again and yet again. This seemed to satisfy the animal's rage. He looked again at his now lifeless foe; appeared quite satisfied with his work, and trotted gaily off, breaking, now and then, into a canter.

Not a soul apparently witnessed this scene except the woman who stood too astonished and terrified to either move or speak. She watched, with terror expressed in her countenance, the disappearing bull. Suddenly she spoke in a whisper: "I know him! It is Apis! Apis, I thank thee for providing me a meal!"

The instinct of the vampire took full possession of her. Her black eyes flamed, her hands opened, her fingers curved like the claws of a bird of prey, and swooping down on the body of the man who had so wildly loved her, she protruded her red lips, and drained the blood from the reeking wounds inflicted by the horns of the bull, while her eyeballs rolled in an ecstasy of delight. At length, gorged to satiety, she dropped from the still bleeding body like a surfeiter leech, and sank back into a lethargic sleep. Meanwhile the corpse of Vincent Cholmondeley, so lately full of life and animated by love and passion, was staring with fixed glazed eyes at the limpid blue sky, while the woman he had so idolised lay close beside it, sound asleep, a seraphic smile playing on her ensanguined lips, like that of a saint in Paradise.

How long the living and the dead lay exposed to the burning rays of the sun, it is impossible to say; but a peasant's cart loomed in the distance later in the day, and lumbered to the foot of the tree near which the two lay extended. The cart stopped, and not a word was spoken by those who descended from it; in fact, an onlooker might have imagined that its arrival on the spot was not a matter of chance; but had been planned beforehand by persons in full possession of all the facts and circumstances of the case. The vehicle contained two brigadiers of the Italian police, men with dark, clearly cut features, shaven faces, cocked hats surmounted with a tall tuft of red, white, and blue, one English detective in plain clothes, and an English hospital nurse.

The driver of the cart, who was clad in ordinary peasant costume, kept his seat, and watched what was going on. Nurse Everest, for it was she, made significant signs to one of the brigadiers to strip the sleeping beauty of her rings before he put on the handcuffs. The man perfectly understood the meaning of her signs, and, kneeling beside the woman, deftly seized the left wrist of the sleeper, and, in a moment, the rings were transferred to his pocket. His next proceeding was to take out the handcuffs, which he adroitly fixed on the delicate white arms of the woman, who was only awakened when she heard the click of the fastening. She opened her black eyes, which in a moment flashed with fury, as she said:

"How dare you, ruffian!" She started to her feet and glared at her captors with the glance of an enraged tigress. "How dare you put manacles on the hands of a lady of my rank and position? What is the cause of this terrible mistake? Take off these handcuffs; and where are my rings? Who has dared to steal them? By what right——"

"*Andiamo, bella mia, non facciamo sciocchezze.*" (Come along, my beauty! Don't let us trifle!)

"Do not dare to touch me, villain! I will not submit to this new indignity. I repeat you are all making a mistake. This poor gentleman has been tossed by a bull, and I fainted at the sight. His death does not lie at my door. Let me pass this instant!"

"Not much, my beauty," replied our old acquaintance, Inspector Jones, speaking for the first time. "Do you remember how cleverly you slipped through my fingers once before? But never again, not if I know it."

"This is a villainous conspiracy," shrieked the woman. Then turning to Nurse Everest she added: "What concern have you in this question? Why are you here?"

"I am here on the part of Sir Ashleigh Carruthers," replied Nurse Everest, calmly facing the enraged woman.

"I know nothing of him. Who is he? It is all a mistake!" the woman replied. Then, turning to the two Italians, she harangued them with such eloquence in their own language that the two men exchanged glances, evidently affected by the looks and words of the beautiful speaker.

"Come, come, a truce to all this fooling," broke in Jones, by way of breaking the spell. Then, turning to the woman, he said, "I beg you, madam, not to hinder us in the discharge of our duty; but to come along quietly, at once."

"Not till my rings are restored to me," she replied firmly.

"All right; then here goes," said the stalwart Jones, and seizing the slim form of the woman in his arms, he thrust her into the cart, while the two brigadiers lifted the dead body of the Englishman, placed it on the floor of the vehicle, and covered it with a piece of tarpaulin. "*Avanti!*" (Forward!) shouted one of the Italians to the driver, who cracked his whip and drove away in the direction of the station house.

• • •

CHAPTER XXXIII

NURSE EVEREST PLAYS
FOR MR. WHIFFLES

◯

In order to explain the appearance of Nurse Everest on the scene, it is necessary to relate what happened on her return to London after her three weeks' holiday. The change had greatly benefited her, and she was well enough to be able to accept a tempting offer that was made to her, to accompany a paralytic patient to the continent. Mr. Whiffles, the patient in question, was a self-made man, who had amassed a colossal fortune in the iron trade, and who had just married the last of his family of daughters. Retiring from business at sixty, he had enjoyed rather too freely the good things of this world, and the result had been, first dyspepsia, and, afterwards, paralysis. His physician had ordered him the simplest diet, entire change of scene, and agreeable society. As he could only move with difficulty, it was necessary that he should be wheeled about in a bath-chair, and have a valet in constant attendance. A man had been recommended by his doctor, who, in addition to his daily duties in which he proved himself efficient, could, if necessary, add to them those of a courier. Mr. Whiffles had no reason to complain of this man; but felt that he required, in addition, someone of the opposite sex, young, healthy, well-bred, and cheerful, to perform those thousand and one delicate little offices which are sometimes comprised under me term "smoothing his pillow for him." The old man was fond of being coddled, when his nurse was young, pretty, and sympathetic, but he would suffer no grim, thin-lipped spinster near him, with a shrewish tone in her voice; neither would he have a large-boned, florid matron, separated from her husband and eager for a profitable engagement, to attend on him. No, our invalid was fastidious about the forms, faces, and disposition of those around him; he had unlimited money, and determined to have exactly what he wanted and nothing else.

His doctor knew Nurse Everest and all her admirable qualities of mind and heart; and, directly Mr. Whiffles glanced at her pretty face and listened to her sweet voice, he eagerly engaged her on the spot, inwardly congratulating himself on his good fortune.

Before departing for the Continent, Nurse Everest wrote to Carruthers informing him of her engagement; adding that she should like to see him before going, as she had some important things to say. As Carruthers had at this time business in London, he arranged to meet her at the Charing Cross Hotel, where they lunched together. Carruthers was very kind and pleasant, and the blush on his companion's face, and the unmistakable light shining in her eyes, were proof of the pleasure she felt in again meeting her former patient. She told her companion that Mr. Whiffles had set his heart on visiting Monte Carlo.

"Why, the very thing!" exclaimed the delighted Carruthers. "Do you know, nurse, that this purpose of your invalid looks like the working of the hand of destiny? Why, that is where she is—the accursed vampire, the Woman in Black!"

"What, you don't mean to tell me, Sir Ashleigh," began the astonished nurse, when Carruthers broke in:

"Yes, I do! I mean distinctly to say that I am perfectly convinced in my own mind that the Russian Princess, who has bewitched my old friend, Cholmondeley, is identical with the abominable Woman in Black, who is living in extravagant style, and whom my deluded friend describes in such glowing terms. I am very much afraid he will marry her; and there is nothing I would not do to save him!"

Both were silent for a few moments, thinking deeply. Carruthers was the first to speak.

"It appears to me to be quite providential that you are now going to Monte Carlo. You can easily make inquiries and let me know, from day to day, the progress of events. Do your best to discover my friend. I myself intend to communicate with the police, and it seems to me, that between us all, it will go hard with the Woman in Black. Of course, until we again possess the magic ring nothing very satisfactory can be done."

"Have you a photograph of your friend, Vincent Cholmondeley?" asked the Nurse.

"Of course I have. What an ass I was not to think of giving it to you before! I will send it to your address on my return home, so that you will have it in your possession before starting."

A long conversation followed, in which notes were compared; Nurse Everest's dreams and visions fully discussed, and, then, it was time to part. And as Carruthers pressed the pretty little hand and looked into the candid blue eyes, he felt an unaccustomed thrill of love pass through his nerves, which quite astonished him and delighted Nurse Everest, who, with true feminine intuition fully realised its depth and value.

When she had gone Carruthers was surprised at his self-restraint in refraining from throwing his arms round the dear little woman and kissing her.

* * * * *

Nurse Everest had been away from England a month, during which time she frequently wrote to Carruthers. Mr. Whiffles was very fond of gambling and visited the saloon every day. The promised photograph had duly reached her, and she looked out eagerly for Carruthers' friend, Vincent Cholmondeley, and soon succeeded in recognising him and the lady who usually accompanied him, the *pseudo* Russian Princess.

Nurse Everest at once realised that it was the creature who had haunted her dreams and visions, the abominable Woman in Black. She knew her beautiful face instantly, although she was no longer dressed in black, but wore the richest and most beautiful garments, and literally blazed with diamonds and the rarest gems. She was followed whenever she appeared by crowds of male worshippers, who hung enthralled on her lightest word.

Amongst the people in the crowded room she noticed a powerful-looking man with a red face and mutton-chop whiskers standing apart and watching every movement of the princess, and his face seemed familiar to Nurse Everest. Where had she seen the man before? After a little thought she remembered him; it was the stalwart Inspector Jones, dressed, of course, in ordinary style. She asked Mr. Whiffles to excuse her for a short time, attracted the attention of Jones, who followed her, and at once remembered her as the nurse who had been in attendance on Carruthers. After a little talk the cautious Jones suggested that it would be safer to appear strangers; but that, of course, he would be ready to give her assistance and advice at any time. Nurse Everest was equally reticent, and did not even admit her patient into her confidence.

One day when play was at its height, Mr. Whiffles had staked a few napoleons and lost, the usual commotion was made in the saloon by the entrance of the Russian Princess, dressed in the most exquisite style, followed by a train of male admirers. "Ah! now we shall see something like play!" said someone in the crowd round the table, and all made way for her."

"Isn't she splendid!" exclaimed another. "*Ach, Gott!*" added a plethoric and bespectacled German with enthusiasm, "I would gif mine right hand to vin her. *Ach!*"

Murmurs of approbation on all sides, and in all tongues, greeted the arrival of this queen of grace and beauty, as she gracefully glided to the gaming table and staked a napoleon.

Mr. Whiffles staked another. The lady won. "Lost again!" muttered the invalid. "Come, nurse," he said, "you have a lucky countenance; you shall play for me." He handed her a napoleon, which she placed on the table.

The Princess staked another, and the nurse won. The loser, who had never in the whole course of her gambling experience lost before, darted a glance of cold amazement at the winner. "Bravo, nurse!" said Mr. Whiffles, as she pocketed the money. "Try again," and he gave her two napoleons. Two were staked by the Princess, and the nurse won again. Mr. Whiffles, through the nurse, staked two more, the Princess did the same, and lost once more.

The Princess thinking this small play monotonous, staked five napoleons.

The nurse received five from Mr. Whiffles, which she staked, and was again the winner.

Of course, the attention of nearly everyone present was concentrated on the good luck of the pretty English hospital nurse. Irritated by her continual ill-fortune, the Princess staked ten napoleons. Mr. Whiffies gave the nurse the same sum, which she staked with the former result.

The beautiful features of the loser began to exhibit decided marks of annoyance; and she increased her stakes again and again, and lost at every venture. Neither being inclined to give way, the play lasted until it was time for the invalid to return to his hotel. He did so, after not only recouping all he had previously lost, but the winner of a few hundred napoleons.

On the following day a repetition of what we have described occurred. The Princess appeared with her usual train of admirers. Again she played heavily, doubling her stakes each time she lost, while Mr. Whiffles, through his lucky nurse, raked in the winnings. This happened every day, the Russian Princess always losing, except now and again, when Mr. Whiffles played on his own account and invariably lost. This continual good luck of the English nurse at the expense of the hitherto always fortunate Russian Princess became the talk of the place, and was spoken of as something extraordinary.

There was one person, however, to whom the fortunes of the gaming table were of quite secondary importance, and that was Inspector Jones. His attention was concentrated on the movements of the lady who masqueraded as a Russian Princess, and whom he had from the beginning identified as the notorious Woman in Black. Jones had, at one time, lived in France for six months, and had picked up a smattering of the language. By this means he had been able to communicate with the Italian police, who nearly all understood French, and had acquainted them with what it was necessary they should know about the mysterious case.

• • •

CHAPTER XXXIV
THE VAMPIRE DIES

C arruthers continued to receive letters from Nurse Everest informing him of what occurred at Monte Carlo. Inspector Jones also communicated with him from time to time. Carruthers chuckled when he heard of the losses of his enemy, not because he thought she would care for the money, for he knew that losing hundreds of thousands would not affect her; but he considered that even her failure at the gaming table proved that, when confronted with Nurse Everest, whom he had enlisted on his side, her supernatural powers deserted her. This appeared to be an auspicious omen, and promised well for the ultimate defeat and destruction of the creature. It was, he thought, a combat between purity and truth *versus* malice, magic, and the Egyptian gods.

After reading a long letter of the nurse's, Carruthers lit his pipe, and thus thought, half aloud: "What a dear girl she is! I believe she would jeopardise her life to serve me. How can I doubt that she loves me! I should be culpably blind not to know it. . . . My feeling for her is unmistakable. She is, in every sense of the term, a lady; not only conventionally, but in mind and heart. . . . and she is the only woman I ever met so constituted as to make me happy. . . . Yes, the more I think of her, the more convinced I feel that I could not be happy without her or with any other woman. . . . Yes, there is no doubt remaining in my mind; and when that horrible woman is disposed of, I will speak."

In the meantime Nurse Everest was racking her brain to discover a way to further the plans of Carruthers by bringing about the arrest of the Woman in Black, and thus prevent her marriage with Vincent Cholmondeley. It did not seem strange to either Carruthers or the nurse that a young man like Cholmondeley should be fascinated by the beauty, arts, and graces of the supposed Russian Princess, set off with all the charm of position, rank, and fashion; but it did appear very astonishing that such a gorgeous adventuress should care to marry an ordinary Englishman destitute of rank and title, with only ordinary wealth, and barely average good looks. It was scarcely possible to believe that she really intended to marry him. If that were so, what could her purpose be in consenting to the union? There could really be only one object, and that was to make of the weak-willed Vincent another victim. As the reader now knows, the Woman in Black could only sustain her horrible existence by copious draughts from time to time of human blood. It was a necessity of her being that hundreds should perish in order that she might prolong indefinitely her accursed form of life. If this did not happen, eternal death was her doom. No hope of a future life loomed in the distance for her. Her existence was only that of the body; the soul had departed long ago; so that death to her meant utter annihilation. Think of it! This terrible doom was ever before her, sharpening all her animal instincts for the purpose of preserving the life that she shuddered at the idea of losing, till those instincts became so acute as to be prophetic.

From the first moment she had looked into the eyes of Nurse Everest, she had felt sure that the woman was destined to stand between her and her cherished existence. This was again felt more deeply when she looked at her on the day of Vincent Cholmondeley's death and her own arrest.

Now we have said that apparently no one witnessed the terrible death of Vincent Cholmondeley and the subsequent abominable feast of blood of the female vampire. This, however, was not the case. What was meant to be understood by the reader was that there appeared to be no living witness of the terrible scene. The lovers had imagined that they were quite alone; and, indeed, so far as anyone being able to help or interfere, they were. It is nevertheless a fact that Nurse Everest, always on the watch for what she felt must happen sooner or later, had followed the two lovers with her eyes from the moment Vincent Cholmondeley left his hotel in the morning; and had at once communicated with Inspector Jones, who had taken a commanding position on a high point in the town, where, unobserved, he himself had watched the pair with a powerful field glass; and thus had been a witness of the entire proceedings from beginning to end, though, unfortunately, he was too far off to prevent the catastrophe.

When Jones beheld the vampire drop off senseless at the conclusion of her abominable repast, he immediately communicated with the Italian police, some of whom started with him and Nurse Everest without delay.

It would be difficult to describe the astonishment and consternation of the inhabitants of Monte Carlo, when they beheld the young and beautiful Russian Princess, the glory of the gambling saloon, the idol of the male sex, and the envy of her own, brought through the streets in a common, jolting, peasant's cart, handcuffed and bloodstained, accompanied by two brigadiers in uniform, Jones and Nurse Everest, on her way to be locked up in a prison cell! Yes, her struggles, her eloquence, her protestations of innocence, and, finally, her tears, were all in vain! No pity was shown to the guilty woman; she was secured in a common cell for the night, in spite of her supposed rank and wealth; and there we will leave her.

After Nurse Everest had attended to all the wants of her patient, she retired at midnight to her own room, which communicated with that of Mr. Whiffles. Her first proceeding was to light a fire in case the invalid should require a cup of tea in the small hours of the morning. The fire in the chimney happened to burn badly, and the nurse found it necessary to open the window to let out the volumes of smoke that filled the room.

After the window had been opened for some time, she heard a sound which appeared like that made by a huge bird beating its wings against the panes; and Nurse Everest wondered what it could be.

The moon was at its full, and shining brilliantly. As she looked up, a black shadow shut out part of the silvery light. A second glance at the object showed her that it was a huge bat furnished with diaphanous wings, through which the moonlight shone as it appeared to pass before the planet's surface. The next instant a monster vampire bat entered the room. In a flash the truth was vividly apparent to Nurse Everest. She had heard of such deadly monsters before, although she had never encountered one. She felt certain that this horrible thing could be nothing but the fell spirit of the witch now lying asleep in the prison cell, which had entered her chamber with the purpose of adding her to the already long list of victims. She knew well how the abominable creature thirsted for her life; and that a deadly and determined struggle for existence was before her. One of them must die, she knew; but she resolved to combat with all her strength; and if she must die to sell her life as dearly as possible. Her first brave impulse was to shut the window, and thus frustrate the brute's retreat. This she did with lightning rapidity; and, then, seizing the poker with her right hand, she stood on the defensive, with the light of battle in her blue eyes.

She watched the monster as it flew round and round the room in circles; coming nearer and nearer to her every time; the red light in its eyes burning brighter and the teeth showing white in the moonlight. Its claws appeared to shoot out and contract, and Nurse Everest felt a numbness steal over the arm holding the poker as if her will power and physical strength were slowly and surely departing. Fully aware that she was being hypnotised by the creature, and that loss of resisting force meant death in the most horrible form, she called forth all her remaining energy, and struck one well-directed blow, which fell with a crash upon the monster's head, causing it to fall on the floor, bleeding profusely. Not yet feeling satisfied with what she had done, Nurse Everest hastened to the brute, which was quivering in its agony, and raised the poker in order to strike another blow, when the creature so far recovered as to fly towards the closed window, seeking an outlet. Failing in this attempt it sank to the floor once more through sheer exhaustion.

Now, no one on earth had a tenderer heart than Nurse Everest; she would not have caused unnecessary pain to any living thing; in fact, her great tenderness of heart had stood in her way at the hospital, where she had been unable to assist at important operations, through her inability to witness the shedding of blood without sickness and fainting. But now she was turned to adamant. No foolish weakness should prevent the execution of the duty she had imposed on herself, *viz.*, the destruction of this abominable monster for the benefit of humanity at large, so raising the poker again, she struck a determined blow which severed its vertebrae.

With a screech and a hiss the monster gazed up at her with a look of impotent hatred, which reminded the nurse of the expression in the face of the woman now secure in her cell. Then laying aside the poker, and seizing the tongs, she grasped the still quivering body, and, in spite of its struggles, she thrust it into the fire, where it frizzled and flamed until the long dreaded monster was reduced to fine white ashes. Not a claw or particle of the body was unconsumed, and the brave little nurse after thus discharging her duty to society, and opening the window to clear the atmosphere, sank senseless on her bed.

•••

CHAPTER XXXV
CONCLUSION

W hen the cell in which the haughty, beautiful, and eloquent prisoner had been confined was entered the next morning, nothing was found there but a charred and unrecognisable corpse, with its spine fractured and its skull cloven. It was at first imagined that the beautiful and overbearing woman had committed suicide to avoid the ignominy of a public trial, by dashing out her brains against the stone wall of her prison; but this hypothesis the doctor, who had been called in, at once declared to be impossible, since she could not have fractured her spine as well as her skull; neither were there any marks on the walls indicating that she had adopted such a desperate course of action. There was a livid, blackened appearance on the body as if it had been struck by lightning; but there had been no storms for weeks past, so that supposition fell to the ground. What could have been the cause of so strange a death? The fracture on the head and the broken spine led to the idea that both had been violently struck with a long weapon of iron or steel; in fact, there seemed no other feasible explanation. Yet who could have dealt the blows? Was it the jailor? He was certainly the last person in the cell with her; and it was not usual for jailors to brutally murder their prisoners. Was it possible that the prisoner had attacked the jailor in a frenzy of rage; and might he, furious with passion, have dealt her two blows with his heavy bunch of keys?

The jailor was questioned; and answered with the nearly unmistakable air of an innocent man. The keys were asked for and carefully examined by the doctor with a magnifying glass, but not the slightest trace of blood could be found on any of them. Had it not been for the deadly wounds the blackened appearance of the body might have suggested poison as the cause of death. After the facts and circumstances had been carefully weighed, all that could be agreed upon was the self-evident fact that the wounds had been inflicted by some person or persons unknown; and there the mystery of the death of the supposed Russian Princess ended. As a matter of course, a certain amount of suspicion rested on the heads of the local police; and they naturally desired to hush the matter up as much, as possible, but their best efforts were ineffectual—it was too good a story to be ignored by the Press—and a long article appeared in the principal paper of Monte Carlo under this heading:

MYSTERIOUS DEATH OF A RUSSIAN ADVENTURESS.

It is unnecessary to give here a repetition of the ghastly details of the story.

Nurse Everest continued to keep her own counsel about her terrible life and death encounter with the vampire bat, with one exception—Inspector Jones, whom she knew she could trust not to reveal more of the revolting details of the case than were necessary. She dreaded lest, after the first burst of public scepticism at so wonderful a tale, people should begin to connect the vampire bat with the witch who had assumed the tide of Russian Princess. The love of the marvellous lies at the root of human nature. Deny it who will, there is concealed somewhere in the depths of the heart of the greatest scoffer, a secret yearning after the unknown. This is especially the case because a knowledge of the unknown is carefully kept from us by those whose interest it is that the unknown should remain the unknown. There is also a prying propensity in human nature—a desire to discover the hidden—which may, in many cases, be defined by only one word—cussedness. With such persons there is no possibility of secrecy, no privacy, no respect for any individual's domestic feelings. Everything must be laid bare to the public gaze, every skeleton must be turned out of its cupboard by those who have taken upon themselves the task of unmasking hypocrisy. On the other hand, it was also from an element of cussedness that Nurse Everest determined that her secret should not become public property.

Inspector Jones shared her feeling in the matter; but there was one other person to whom the secret must be revealed; and, the morning after the dread experience, Nurse Everest penned a full description of it to Ashleigh Carruthers; and in addition, gave him a full account of the tragic death of his old friend, Vincent Cholmondeley. Jones wired to Carruthers, and afterwards wrote him a long letter.

Carruthers telegraphed to Jones to make all arrangements for the burial of Cholmondeley, and added that he would start for Monte Carlo without delay. In the shortest possible time Carruthers was on the spot. He arrived too late to see the face of his old friend, the coffin having been screwed down before he reached the place. Carruthers did not stay longer than necessary, and returned to England with the remains of his unfortunate friend, which were interred in the family vault of the Cholmondeleys.

As for the charred body of the Woman in Black, it received no honoured burial, but was put under the earth in some sequestered corner, few knew where. No stone marked the spot, no relation or friend followed her, who had been outside the pale of humanity, and had, indeed, been a scourge and a curse. On the contrary, those who had heard and believed in the mysterious reports about her, gave a sigh of relief at her departure, and felt themselves safer.

When inquiries were made at the Russian Consulate by the police authorities at Monte Carlo, they were informed that no such titles as that assumed by the deceased woman had ever existed; that she was evidently not a Russian at all; neither could her origin be traced. Under such circumstances, her vast wealth in gold, jewellery, and securities, amounting to millions, from no one knew what source, was claimed by the Italian Government. When Carruthers represented to the head of the administration at Monte Carlo that he was himself chiefly interested in the late *soi-disant* Russian Princess, and added that he alone could throw light on her past, the official appeared greatly interested in what he related; and, after a long interview, as a memento of the conversation, gave Carruthers the long coveted magic ring.

Armed with this potent charm, he departed for England, and, after seeing the body of his friend buried, had visited his old nurse Sarah, and told her the story of the Woman in Black.

But before leaving Monte Carlo a very important event occurred, for which we think the reader is quite prepared. We refer to the meeting between Carruthers and Nurse Everest. It is unnecessary to say how deeply Carruthers admired the dauntless courage and determination she had displayed. He also appreciated all her delightful feminine qualities; her splendid talent for silence; her sweet voice, her sleepless vigilance when pain or care could be mitigated; in short, her kind heart and delightful tact.

Carruthers had the good sense to make her an offer of his hand and heart, which she, after some hesitation, accepted. He made his offer like a man who had made up his mind to win her; and who had looked at the question from all sides. Nurse Everest, as we will still term her, pointed out to him, with perfect frankness, the difference in their positions and social standing. Carruthers replied that she could say nothing on that score, that he had not weighed in his own mind with the most careful consideration; that she was a lady by birth and education; and, over and above that, she, in mind, temper, and character, was exactly the woman who could make him happy. Nurse Everest looked into his keen grey eyes, and did justice to the determination expressed by his straight, firm mouth and square jaw, and fully realising that to accept him, and, at the same time, satisfy the ardent desire of her own heart, was the only course to pursue, put her little hand in his; and, as if by instinct, their lips met in a warm kiss.

When her engagement with Mr. Whiffles terminated, she returned to England; and, shortly after, the congregation at the parish church of Little Fuddleton were nearly startled out of their wits by hearing the old vicar make the following statement: "I publish the banns of marriage between Ashleigh Carruthers, bachelor, of this parish, and Celia Agnes Macullum, spinster, of this parish.... This is the first time of asking. If any person knows any just cause or impediment why these parties should not be joined together in holy matrimony, ye are to declare it."

"I stop it!" called out a solitary voice, proceeding from a plethoric local dignitary who had risen to his feet.

Every head was turned towards the objector in wonder, whilst whispering and tittering came from the ladies.

The minister invited the protestor to make his objection in the vestry at the close of the service. The service was continued, and Carruthers, who was present, treated the outburst with indifference, merely looking at the stout gentleman with an amused smile. After the service, several acquaintances of Carruthers tried to waylay him, hoping to extract material for gossip; but he carefully escaped their attentions, and quickly jumping into his carriage, escaped. There was, naturally, much conjecture as to what the objection could be which threatened to frustrate Carruthers' marriage. Some ladies were of the opinion that he was already married; others thought he had half a dozen wives living. But all this was nothing but gossip; and the local magnate's protest was found to be based only on his bare assertion that Carruthers had paid attention to one of his daughters; as many charitable persons asserted he had done to other ladies, so that no real obstacle stood in the way of the union.

The wedding day was propitious, and the fair bride looked charming, as did the bridesmaids. Lady Ashleigh Carruthers, after the ceremony, left the church on the arm of her husband, to become mistress of Tudor Hall, and the envy of nearly all the unmarried ladies in the county. Their honeymoon was spent on the Continent, chiefly in the south of Europe, but Monte Carlo did not form one of their resting-places, as the reader would readily understand. On their return home, they were warmly welcomed by the best families in the district, and it was not long before the natural charm of Lady Carruthers' character made her a general favourite. Her former career rendered her ministrations to the poor and sick extremely valuable, and she was soon adored by them. She was always true to her beautifully balanced nature— unaffected, natural, well-bred, intelligent, and loving. Sir Ashleigh found reason to congratulate himself on the wise, unconventional choice he had made. His wife was a perfect hostess, an excellent nurse, a delightful companion, and, later on, an exemplary mother.

* * * * *

"But what became of the magic ring?" the reader will probably enquire. Finding themselves haunted by the Egyptian deities who guarded the treasure, and feeling that they both could dispense with their attentions, the ring was sent to the British Museum, where it remains to the present day.

• • •